Dark River Legacy

DAYBREAK MYSTERY

B·J·HOFF

ACCENT BOOKS
CHARIOT FAMILY PUBLISHING
A DIVISION OF DAVID C. COOK PUBLISHING CO.

Accent Books™ is an imprint of David C. Cook Publishing Co.
David C. Cook Publishing Co., Elgin, Illinois 60120
David C. Cook Publishing Co., Weston, Ontario
Nova Distribution Ltd., Newton Abbot, England

DARK RIVER LEGACY
©1990 by B.J. Hoff

Cover design by Koechel/Peterson & Associates
First Printing, 1990
Printed in the United States of America
96 95 94 93 92 6 5 4 3 2

Library of Congress Catalog Card Number 88-70756
ISBN 0-7814-0479-7

FOR RETA,
My mother . . .
For her, the Lord
has always been enough . . .

OTHER ACCENT BOOKS BY B.J. HOFF:

Mists of Danger

Daybreak Mystery Series:
      Storm at Daybreak
      The Domino Image
      The Tangled Web
      Vow of Silence
      Dark River Legacy

When yesterday's bright dreams
dissolve to dust,
the Lord stands waiting
with outstretched hands
to offer better things . . .
When everything in which
we've placed our trust
begins to crumble,
there's still One who never fails—
the King of Kings . . .

B.J. Hoff
from *Banners*

Prologue

He was an immense column of a man, but in his black clothing, he blended easily with the night. Even his white hair was concealed, except for the burred front, by a black shooter's cap.

He moved steadily, almost woodenly, up the hillside, his thick-pillared legs spanning several feet at a time. He carried an AK-47 rifle on a sling and wore a 9mm Beretta with a silencer on a belt slide. Concealed in an ankle rig was a .38 Bulldog. A pair of Israeli-designed infrared goggles dangled from a neck strap, tapping his massive chest as he climbed.

The small white cabin just up the hill was dark except for a dim glow, which he assumed to be a night light, seeping from a rear window. It came on every night a little after eleven, only a moment after all the other inside lights went out. At the same time, the outside security light mounted on a pole left of the cabin would go on, beaming a pinkish-gold spray across part of the side and most of the front yard.

He had been watching the cabin for four nights, and the routine hadn't varied more than a few minutes one way or the other.

The old lady might be loony-tunes, but she was predictable.

It was a sultry night, sticky with late spring humidity and sweet with the mix of wild flowers. He slapped automatically at a prickle on his heavily muscled upper arm; the bugs had

7

been after him since sunset, and he was beginning to wish he'd worn a long-sleeved shirt, regardless of the heat.

He climbed a few more feet, then stopped. With one hand on the stock of the rifle and the other splayed at his waist, he stood, watching.

The cabin had the look of a little girl's playhouse. A neat flagstone walk traced the path to the front steps. Frilly curtains trimmed the small, square windows, and a calico wreath hung on the door. The front edge of the porch was lined with a variety of flowering potted plants.

His mind replayed his orders: Isolate her, question her, terminate her. If she appeared to be even halfway rational—if there were a chance, no matter how slight, that she might have spilled anything about the *Lady A*—he was also to eliminate her entire circle of acquaintances. They couldn't afford the risk that the old diz might have talked or, if she hadn't yet remembered, might at some point in the future.

From what he'd seen so far, she wasn't tight with anyone except the teacher who lived down the hill from her, and he'd be easy enough to settle. He seemed to spend most of his time roaming around the woods or rapping with the college kids along the riverbank.

Just to be safe, he'd watch another two or three days before making his move. Not so much to nail down her routine—he was pretty sure of it by now—but more to make certain there was no one else in her life, someone he might have missed. Someone she might have talked to.

He decided to take care of the security light, to make things easier when he was ready.

Removing the silenced Beretta from his belt, he aimed, fired once, and waited. The light popped with the first shot, and after a couple of seconds he replaced the automatic in the slide and turned to start back down the hill.

Without a backward glance, he retraced the same route he'd followed on the way up, veering right after a few yards to start around the ridge. He continued to walk until he reached an abandoned storage shed and a black van, both nearly obscured by a dense cover of trees.

Abby woke up slowly, blinking as her eyes attempted to focus. The room was quiet except for Peaches' soft purring at the foot of the bed and the rhythmic ticking of the alarm clock on the night table. She had left the window air conditioner turned on, but it wasn't running.

For several moments she lay unmoving. The darkness of the bedroom was relieved only by the faint glow of a night light plugged into the wall outlet. Beyond the open doorway, the hall was dark.

She pushed herself up on one arm, grimacing at the dull ache in her lower back as she moved. Reaching for her glasses with fingers stiff from sleep and arthritis, she put them on and squinted at the clock's luminescent hands.

Almost midnight. She frowned, remained propped on her side, thinking.

What had awakened her? Not that it was unusual for her to wake up several times during the night. She'd never been a sound sleeper. At least she didn't think she had been. She couldn't remember the Time-Before-the-Hospital, but since she'd come to the mountain, she was often restless at night.

Sometimes she dreamed. Dark, cavernous dreams that wound through endless tunnels and shadowed chambers. Often she awoke frightened and bewildered, her heart pounding with an urgency to remember . . . something.

But the dreams would fade after she'd been awake for awhile, and she would firmly put aside any trace of lingering uneasiness.

She sighed, and the small cat sleeping at her feet stirred and yawned, but didn't get up.

After another moment, she lifted a hand to remove her

9

glasses, then stopped.

A cold finger of apprehension touched the nape of her neck, warning her that things weren't quite as they should be.

Something was wrong. Leaving her glasses on, Abby turned toward the window at the head of the bed.

The faint golden rays from the security light usually filtered through the curtains, but now there was only a thick, inky darkness.

Flipping back the sheet, she pushed herself up, sitting on the side of the bed until the pain in her back ebbed. Then she got up and went to the window. Lifting one corner of the ruffled yellow curtain, she peered outside.

Nothing. She pulled the curtain back a little more, but could still see nothing except thick, obscure shadows.

The security light was out. Now when had that happened? It had been on when she went to bed, she was sure.

She gave another sigh, turning back toward the bed when she heard a soft, questioning mew from Peaches.

The small, orange-spotted cat stood up, stretched, then stood staring at her owner.

"Our outside light is burned out, Peaches. Of course, that probably doesn't bother you at all, does it? You could see just fine out there, with or without the light, couldn't you? But I don't believe I care for it very much. Tomorrow we'll ask Mitch if he'll replace it for us. I'm sure he will, he—"

Abby jumped back when the air-conditioner suddenly switched on and churned to life, then shook her head at her own foolishness.

"My, I'm as nervous as a cat—excuse me, Peaches— jumping at every noise. Goodness, there's nothing to be afraid of up here, is there, no matter how dark it is?"

She glanced out the window once more, then turned, put her glasses on the night table, and went back to bed.

At her feet, Peaches padded around in a circle a couple of

times before settling back into the nest she'd made earlier. After washing her face with her front paws, she curled up in a ball and closed her eyes.

1

Jennifer thought Derry Ridge, Kentucky must be about as far removed from life in the fast lane as an Amish farm would be from Times Square. It was a setting that invited contentment, a place that enticed you to relax a little and dream a lot.

The hillside across the river from the campus was a deep, lush green, the May woods spotted with pink and yellow flowering shrubs. The air was spiced with the rich smells of things blooming and growing in fertile soil. Even the sounds around them hinted of new beginnings and fresh hope. Birds sang as they built their nests; honey bees buzzed a counter melody while they raced one another for the choicest pot of pollen; and in the background was the ever present harmony of the Derry River, running clean and strong and constant.

Jennifer yawned, then gave a long, feline stretch as she turned to look at her drowsy husband. She smiled at what she saw. Daniel's eyes were closed, his chin lifted toward the early afternoon sun. A soft haze of gold and flickering shadows dappled the strong lines of his face. Sunny, his guide dog, lay peacefully at her master's feet, her paws nestled snugly under her chin.

"It's incredibly beautiful here, Daniel."

"Mm-hm."

"I wish you could see it, especially the colors. They're"— Jennifer searched for a description he could visualize clearly—"Easter egg colors."

One eyebrow quirked a little. "Mm."

Half-asleep, just as she'd suspected. "I think this must be what Scotland or Ireland looks like in the spring. No wonder

Mitch goes on so about his home state."

Daniel nodded.

"You know, he isn't quite what I expected."

Daniel slouched a little deeper against the picnic bench, stretching his long legs even further out in front of him. "How's that?" It was a halfhearted question.

"I think I expected him to be more"—she stopped to think—"more *intellectual.* You know—bookish? Maybe a little forgetful."

It was Daniel's turn to yawn. With obvious reluctance, he sat up, ran a hand over the back of his neck, then slipped his arm around her shoulder. "The absent-minded professor stereotype?"

"Yes, I suppose so. He's certainly proved me wrong."

For a moment, she returned her attention to their surroundings. Across the grounds to her right, the chapel clock struck two but was muffled by a large group of boisterous young people making their way from the Student Center to the parking lot.

"He seems awfully *tense,* don't you think?"

"Maybe a little." He paused, then added, "He did walk the floor most of last night."

Surprised, Jennifer turned to look at him. "If you heard him, then you weren't sleeping either."

He shrugged, brushing a gnat away from his arm. "You know I never sleep much the first night away from home."

Abruptly, she sat up. "You don't suppose there's something wrong, do you? Maybe we should have stayed at the Lodge after all."

Daniel shook his head. "He wouldn't even discuss it. Ever since we agreed to do the workshop, he's insisted that we stay with him. I imagine he's just keyed up about this festival. Coordinating the whole thing has to be a lot of work."

"I hope that's all it is," she said, again resting her head on his shoulder. "He seems awfully nice. And gentle. I think he's a very gentle man." She tilted her head to look up at him. "I wonder why he's not married yet."

Daniel shook his head, grinning. "You have a real problem with the idea of a man over thirty who's still single, don't you darlin'?"

"Most men are married by the time they're thirty, Daniel," she reminded him archly.

"I wasn't."

"That's different. You were waiting for me."

"Smartest decision I ever made, too," he said agreeably.

"Mm. Well, maybe he's engaged," she said, somewhat distracted by her study of Daniel's profile.

"Mitch? I don't think so. He's never mentioned anyone special, and the way I sometimes go on about you, I imagine he'd say something if he had a lady in his life."

Pleased, she smiled to herself. "Odd. He's so nice, I would have thought—"

She stopped when she glanced across the lawn and saw the subject of their conversation walking toward them. "Here he comes now," she cautioned Daniel.

Mitch Donovan crossed the grounds with an easy, ambling stride, but Jennifer sensed the same undercurrent of tension hovering about him that she'd felt at their first meeting the day before.

A tall, rangy man in his early thirties, he approached with his head down, his shoulders hunched slightly forward as if burdened by an invisible weight. His curly, dark-copper hair had trapped a spray of sunshine and appeared to be shot with gold dust in a fiery, glistening contrast to his much darker beard.

Daniel had met the professor from Kentucky at a youth rally in Clarksburg two years earlier. Their mutual interest in music, particularly Appalachian folk and contemporary Christian music, had launched a long-distance friendship.

15

As the director of the "Kentucky Heritage Department," Mitch coordinated an annual Heritage Arts Festival. Each year the week-long event focused on a different kind of music, offering workshops and concerts by various artists. This year, contemporary Christian music was to be featured, and Mitch had invited the Kaines to lead one of the workshops.

Knowing that her own invitation was merely a courtesy didn't bother Jennifer in the least. She simply applauded Mitch's good sense in recognizing the contribution that Daniel could make to the Festival. Daniel had begun to gain widespread attention as a gifted composer in his own right. *Daybreak*, a musical drama he'd written after being blinded, had met with astonishing success; its title song was still frequently recorded by numerous artists. More recently, the popular husband-and-wife team of Paul Alexander and Vali Tremayne had been recording a number of Daniel's songs on their albums, all of which were rapidly rising to the top of the Christian music charts.

Now that they were here, Jennifer was more enthusiastic than ever about the week ahead. The workshops should be fun, and she was excited about the prospect of meeting some of the celebrities who would be in attendance. *Lifestream,* one of the most popular singing groups in the Christian music industry—and a favorite of Daniel's—was expected on Friday. But she was far more excited about another guest, one who had nothing to do with music.

The brochure Mitch had mailed them just last week had featured an announcement that the internationally acclaimed novelist, Gwynevere Leigh—"America's First Lady of Mystery"—would be returning to her hometown to lead a creative writing workshop during the Festival.

Jennifer was determined to meet the young author who had stunned the publishing world with two best-selling novels before she graduated from college. She had packed her brand new copy of Leigh's most recent book with the hope of having it autographed.

All things considered, the week promised to be one to remember.

"All things considered," Mitch abruptly announced in a grim tone of voice as he came to stand in front of them, "this week promises to be a real challenge."

Jennifer sat up, glancing at him with surprise. "Is something wrong, Mitch?"

Noisily jingling a ring of keys in his hand, he glanced back over his shoulder at the river for a moment before answering. When he turned, his expression was one of concern.

"I was counting on being able to have all the concerts and at least a few of the workshops outdoors," he explained. "Our auditorium is too small for the concert attendance we get, and last year we had standing room only in some of the workshops, too. But I just heard the weather forecast for the week."

"Bad?" Daniel yawned, then straightened and got to his feet.

"Miserable. Rain most of the week. *Heavy* rain. Starting tomorrow."

"They're not always right," Daniel offered, slipping his hands into his pants pockets. "Maybe it'll change directions."

"Let's hope."

Jennifer stood up. "Mitch, since you're in charge this week, do you think you could do me a favor?"

Pocketing the ring of keys, he smiled at her. "I'll surely try. What do you need?"

"I'm a big fan of Gwynevere Leigh. Do you think you could arrange for me to meet her? At least long enough to get an autograph? I couldn't believe it when I saw that she's going to be here this week—and that she used to *live* here! Did you know her?"

Puzzled, Jennifer saw his smile fade. The lean angles of his

17

face seemed to tense, and the glint of amusement ordinarily dancing in his eyes disappeared.

He blinked, started to answer her, then hesitated. Gradually his expression cleared. "I . . . used to know her, yes. Well enough to get you an autograph, anyway."

"Wonderful!"

Avoiding her gaze, Mitch changed the subject. "We'd better get the two of you acquainted with the campus while the sun's still shining. Feel like taking a walk?" Without waiting for a reply, he put a hand on Daniel's shoulder. "Why don't we start with Johnson Hall? That's where your workshop will be if it rains."

They spent the next hour becoming familiar with the campus. Mitch was an enthusiastic guide; his love for the college and the town of Derry Ridge obviously ran deep. Jennifer also sensed that his relationship with other members of the faculty and the student body was one of mutual respect and affection. There was a spontaneous, uninhibited warmth that seemed to run between the young professor and everyone they encountered on their tour.

"Let's head toward the cafeteria," he said as they left the language arts building. "I could do with some coffee."

"How do you keep so many students on campus this time of year?" Daniel asked, stopping at the edge of a curb with Sunny. "The semester's over, isn't it?"

"Actually, most of them wouldn't miss this week," Mitch explained as Daniel stepped down. "Almost the entire student body either stays on campus or comes back for the Festival. It's become a tradition."

"Take a right after we get across the parking lot, Dan," Mitch said, watching as Sunny nudged Daniel out of the way of a loose chunk of concrete lying in his path. "Does Sunny handle crowds pretty well? It's probably going to get crazy by tomorrow."

"She'll be fine," Daniel replied, stepping up onto the

18

sidewalk and turning right, as Mitch had directed. "Seeing Eye dogs get plenty of training in crowd control before they graduate. Sunny's a people dog."

"She's a beauty, too," Mitch observed, smiling at the retriever.

"She makes a big difference in my life," Daniel acknowledged. He paused a beat, then grinned. "Just like my other lady."

"Nice of you to include me," Jennifer said dryly.

Unexpectedly, Mitch stopped. "Well, now, here comes the special lady in *my* life," he said, smiling and lifting a hand in greeting.

Pleased by the revelation that there was a woman in Mitch's life after all, Jennifer turned to look. It took her a moment to realize that the subject of Mitch's attention was a diminutive, round-faced woman who looked to be in her mid-sixties. Glancing back at Mitch, she saw his smile warm even more as the woman hurried up to them.

"Mitch! Oh, I'm so glad I finally found you!" The small, plump woman was clearly agitated, her words tumbling out in a rush as she clenched and unclenched her hands in front of her.

"They said you were in the chapel, but you weren't." Stopping only two or three inches away from him, she let her head fall back in order to look up into Mitch's face.

He stooped slightly, enough to make it easier for her accusing blue eyes to meet his as he smiled down at her. "What's the matter, Abby? Peaches didn't run off again, did she?"

"Peaches?" The woman looked at him blankly for a moment. "Oh, no. No, Peaches is at home, Mitch. I was afraid to let her out this morning."

Mitch frowned. "Afraid to let her out? Why?"

"Because of what happened last night. I was afraid she'd get hurt."

19

"Last night? What happened last night?"

Abby visibly relaxed the moment Mitch took her by the hand.

"That's what I'm trying to tell you, Mitch." She had a rose-blossom mouth that trembled slightly as her words poured out in a fast-flowing stream. "That's why I didn't come to church this morning. Did you look for me?"

He nodded. "I did, yes, but by the time I went downstairs with the choir and got out of my robe, I figured you'd already left. Now, what's this about last night? What happened?"

"I don't like it, Mitch! I don't like it at all. It was probably one of those vandals you told me about, playing a trick on me, but it made me nervous."

Mitch's gaze roamed over the woman's tousled, gray-blonde hair, then scanned the circle of her face. A pretty face, Jennifer noted, wide-eyed and sweet despite the inexpertly applied makeup. It was the kind of face you would instinctively trust, she thought, with features reminiscent of a gentle-voiced grandmother or a favorite, warm-hearted aunt. She wondered about her place in Mitch's life.

"Abby, tell me what happened." Mitch's voice was kind, his affection for the woman impossible to miss.

"The security light outside the cabin, Mitch—it's completely shattered. I think somebody shot it out."

"Shot it out?" Mitch's pleasant, good-humored expression suddenly turned hard. "When?"

"Last night," Abby said with obvious impatience. "Didn't I just tell you that, dear? Will you fix it for me, Mitch?"

After a couple of seconds, he nodded distractedly. "Sure, I'll fix it," he answered, still holding her hand. "Abby, do you have any idea what time this happened? Did you see anyone?"

Calmer now, Abby shook her head. "No. I woke up a little before midnight, and when I looked out there wasn't a bit of light. The only thing I found this morning was a lot of glass

20

around the bottom of the pole."

She paused, darting an almost apologetic glance toward Jennifer and Daniel before going on in a quieter tone of voice. "It's awfully dark outside without that light, Mitch. Do you think you could fix it soon?"

Frowning, Mitch hesitated. "I don't think I can get a replacement before tomorrow, Abby."

Her face crumpled.

"It's Sunday, sweetheart," Mitch reminded her gently. "I can't get what I need today." He paused. "I tell you what; I have a floodlight we can hook up this evening, until I can get a replacement for the pole lamp. It'll do almost as well. All right?"

Jennifer was unable to stop a smile of her own as Abby's face smoothed to a pleased smile of relief. "I knew you'd think of something, Mitch," she said, reaching up to pat his lean, bearded face with a chubby hand. "You always do."

Mitch grinned down at her, then gave her a hug. "Come over here, I want you to meet some friends. Remember, I told you about Daniel and Jennifer, that they'd be staying with me this week?"

Abby already seemed to know a great deal about the Kaines. "But where's your little boy?" she asked abruptly after the introductions had been made. "Didn't he come too?"

When Jennifer explained that Jason was staying with Daniel's family for the week, Abby's chin dropped dejectedly. "Oh dear, and I made *cookies* for him. Chocolate chip and peanut butter and pineapple crunch and. . .oh, well. . . ."

Moving in a little closer, Daniel flashed a hopeful smile in Abby's direction. "In Jason's absence, Abby, I'd be happy to help get rid of those cookies."

She beamed up at him. "Well, now, you can have just as many as you want, Daniel. I've made hundreds this week, for the fellowship time after the concerts. And for Mitch, too, of course."

21

Pausing for only a quick breath, Abby turned her attention to Jennifer. "Aren't you terribly proud of your husband, dear? I have a tape of *Daybreak* and a Vali Tremayne tape with some of Daniel's songs on it. He writes such beautiful music, doesn't he? I listen to music all the time, and I simply love Daniel's."

She caught another quick puff of breath before rushing on. "Mitch promised to bring you to visit this week. My cabin is just up the hill from his. Mitch and some of his young people fixed it up for me, painted it inside and out—it's just like new. He's wonderfully handy," she added in a soft, conspiratorial tone, "for a musician."

Delighted with her, Jennifer pressed Daniel's arm and saw him grin in response.

"Well, dear," Abby said, turning back to Mitch, "I have to run. Mrs. Snider is waiting for me in the cafeteria."

"You're working this afternoon?" Mitch asked. "You weren't in there at lunchtime, were you?"

"No, no, I just came down to help get the macaroni salad and baked beans ready for tomorrow, so we don't have to do it later. I want to hear your choir tonight."

After Mitch had reassured her one more time that he'd take care of an outside light for her that evening, Abby bustled off, all signs of her earlier anxiety gone.

"She's *wonderful!*" Jennifer exclaimed, watching Abby bounce down the concrete walk. "Are the two of you related?"

Smiling fondly as he watched Abby disappear through the cafeteria entrance of the Student Center, Mitch shook his head. "No, no relation. We just kind of—adopted each other. As a matter of fact, nobody really knows who Abby is. Or where she came from."

Curious, Jennifer kept her hand on Daniel's arm as they started to walk toward the sprawling brick Student Center. "She's not from here then?"

22

"No. She just started showing up on campus every day several months ago. She'd walk around the grounds and talk to the students; sometimes she'd slip into the back of the chapel for worship and then leave as soon as it was over. One of the counselors found out she was living like a bag lady in an equipment shed up on the hill behind the girls' dorms. Eventually, the senior class and some of the faculty took her under their wings and fixed up a little abandoned cabin for her, just up the Ridge from my place. She's been living there ever since."

"You don't know where she came from?" asked Daniel.

Mitch shook his head. "No idea. We don't even know her last name. *She* doesn't know it."

The memory of Abby's sweetly attractive face with its guileless smile nagged at Jennifer. What could have forced a woman like that into such destitute circumstances?

"Amnesia?" Daniel asked, his interest obviously piqued.

Mitch hesitated, then nodded. "Apparently. Although she does remember a few things. She told us that she came here on a bus; she remembered being in a hospital somewhere, but she doesn't know where it was. Sometimes she seems to remember things about a room she spent a lot of time in—a room with light blue walls and a painting of a dove."

Daniel stopped walking, bringing Jennifer up short with him. "Did you try to trace her background?"

"The local police supposedly put out some queries on her, but with our police department . . . ." With a shrug, he let his words die away, unfinished.

"What do you suppose this business with her yard light means?"

Mitch looked worried. "We've had a lot of vandalism around town for the past year or so. Most of it from teenagers, I'm afraid. Our dropout rate is high all over the county—a lot of kids are getting in trouble just because they

23

don't seem to have anything else to do. I'll call the police about it, but I doubt if they'll be able to find out anything."

"You said Abby remembered something about a hospital," Daniel remarked thoughtfully. "Had she been ill, do you think?"

"She seemed perfectly all right to me. Oh, some of the people in town think she's—odd—but I don't buy that. She's a little flighty, maybe—forgetful sometimes. But the administration gave her a job in the cafeteria, and she was practically running the place in a few weeks. She can be efficient when she has to be. It seems to me that the only thing wrong with Abby is that she's apparently had a few rough breaks in her life."

Jennifer studied Mitch's profile as he and Daniel talked. He had a good face, she decided. A kind and sensitive, caring face. She felt instinctively that he was a good man.

But not an altogether happy man. In spite of the laugh lines that creased the corners of those deep-set, golden-brown eyes, his gaze was vulnerable—and not entirely trusting.

"The one thing we *do* know for certain about Abby," Mitch was saying, "is that she's a Christian. She had a small Bible with her, and she's well-acquainted with its contents." A soft smile crossed his face. "She may not know a thing about where she came from—but she knows exactly where she's going. You know, one of the Bible professors here has a saying that I think relates pretty well to Abby: 'You have to get to the point where Jesus Christ is all you *have* before you realize that Jesus Christ is all you *need*.'"

Still smiling, he added quietly, "As far as Abby's concerned, she's got everything she needs. And a lot more than money can buy."

"Speaking of what money can buy—" Jennifer interrupted, her attention caught by a sleek, silver Mercedes easing into a

24

parking space on the opposite side of the lot.

The door on the driver's side opened, and as Jennifer stared in unabashed admiration, a slender, raven-haired young woman stepped out of the car. Straightening, she took a long, thorough look at her surroundings.

Jennifer heard Mitch catch a sharp breath and turned to look at him. His face was ashen; his hands at his sides trembled noticeably. He looked like a man who had just witnessed a major disaster.

Again Jennifer's gaze went to the driver of the Mercedes. She was tall, taller than Jennifer's five-eight, and willow-slim in a flamboyant peasant dress that would have been outrageous on anyone else. A riot of long, glossy black hair emphasized the pale oval of a face that, even from a distance of several yards, was a striking display of high cheekbones and enormous eyes.

It took Jennifer another moment to realize why the face was so familiar: she had seen it on numerous book jackets. "That's *her*!"

Daniel lifted one dark, questioning brow. "Who?"

Instead of answering, Jennifer turned excitedly to Mitch. "That *is* Gwynevere Leigh, isn't it?"

The generous curve of Mitch's mouth had tightened to a hard line. A peculiar, almost feverish glint burned behind his eyes, and he took a sudden, jerky step backward as if he were about to turn and run. Finally, after what appeared to be an enormous struggle, he expelled a long breath and answered Jennifer. "Yes, that's her."

At that moment the woman turned toward them. She stood unmoving for a long time, her eyes locked on Mitch. At last, she began to walk, slowly at first, then a little faster, her gaze never leaving Mitch's face as she approached.

Jennifer thought she could almost hear the crackle of electricity arcing between Mitch and the striking young author as she walked toward them.

She stopped in front of Mitch. Lifting her chin in a gesture that seemed oddly defiant—and in direct contrast to her uncertain smile—she studied him for a long, silent moment.

Her voice was surprisingly soft when she spoke. "Hello, Mitch." She seemed to hold her breath once the words were out.

Jennifer looked at Mitch. He appeared to be having difficulty swallowing but otherwise seemed to have regained control. The only sign of his earlier discomfiture was the faint glaze of pain in his eyes.

"Hello, Freddi," he said quietly after an awkward silence. "Welcome home."

Jennifer's curiosity reluctantly gave way to consideration as she saw the look that passed between them. Pressing Daniel's arm to indicate that an exit was in order, she began to move. "Let's get some coffee, Daniel," she said, realizing that no one except her husband was aware she had spoken.

2

He had rehearsed this scene in his mind a hundred times or more since learning that she was coming back, but not once had he come close to anticipating the brutal, dizzying pain that now ripped through him.

For a moment Mitch thought he was going to make a total fool of himself, feeling a desperate, childish desire to turn and run. Instead, he could only stand gawking at her, drinking in the sight of her, wildly attempting to still the violent storm raging inside his head.

It was as if he were eighteen all over again—eighteen and hopelessly, helplessly, foolishly in love.

The years, it seemed, hadn't really passed at all. It had been only a dream, a cruel, mocking dream, those dismal years without her. Time couldn't have passed. It must have merely hung suspended. Nothing had changed. She hadn't changed. . .not all that much. She was thinner. Too thin. But she still had style.

She had always had style. Even in a baseball cap and sweatshirt she'd had a kind of elegant-boned, unconventional flair, a distinct panache that made her. . .Freddi.

Strange, how naturally the affectionate little pet name he'd given her in junior high had spilled from his lips. It occurred to him that the unmistakably chic Gwynevere Leigh might resent being referred to as *Freddi.*

And yet, it still seemed to fit her.

"You're looking good, Mitch."

She was looking like yesterday. The long sweep of midnight-silk hair still framed a fair, dew-fresh complexion. The nose still turned up a little too much to be perfect, and the deep gray eyes were still unnervingly steady and measuring. As he remembered, she wore no makeup; the faint blush touching her cheeks and lips was natural.

Her grandfather had sometimes fondly called her *Snow White,* and Mitch had found the comparison intriguingly appropriate, occasionally echoing it.

"And that makes you my prince," she would archly reply.

A pain knifed through him, the kind of pain he hadn't felt since those long, punishing months after she'd gone. He felt himself sway and hoped she hadn't noticed.

Dimly aware that he needed to say something, he moistened his lips and ventured thickly, "How have you been?"

Now that's an opener with real punch, Donovan. . . maybe you should have been a writer, too. . . .

There was the grin. That impish, gently taunting grin with its saucy hint of challenge, its faint tilt of mischief. Was it a shade less confident now, or was he only imagining the unfamiliar softness around her mouth?

She surprised him by giving an uncertain little shrug and a short, "Okay. At least I will be after my stomach stops heaving."

He stared at her blankly.

She glanced over her shoulder, toward the parking lot and the highway beyond. "Some creep in a black van ran me off the road. I just about went over the drop at the dam trying to get out of his way."

He was finding it difficult to hear her, to comprehend her words. His head was swollen with the sight of her, his mind locked in place. "Are you all right?"

She tossed off his question with an indifferent wave of her hand. "Just aggravated." She looked at him. "So, Mitch— you're a full professor now."

He nodded. Even her voice was the same. Soft but direct, poised but with a hint of amusement lurking just below the

28

surface, as if at any moment she might break into that full-throated laugh of hers that always made anyone nearby laugh with her.

He hadn't believed she would come, had made an awkward attempt to dissuade the language arts committee from inviting her. Even when he heard that she'd accepted, he had been so sure she'd back out at the last minute. *If only she had. . .*

He looked back at her to find her studying his face with an intensity that made his throat tighten and close.

"That's what you always wanted. I'm glad for you, Mitch."

What I always wanted was you, Freddi. . .more than anything else. . .and you knew it.

He tried to force a smile, felt instead a rictus of pain slash his mouth as he groped to slide a mask of composure into place.

"This is a surprise," he finally managed, "seeing you here."

"You didn't know I was coming?"

"I knew," he said too quickly. "I just wasn't sure—"

"That I'd show up?" she finished for him, her wide, high brows lifting speculatively.

He shrugged his answer. "Will you be here . . . all week?" He made himself meet her eyes, felt his control start to slip away again.

She looked back at him, unhurriedly studying his face before answering. "Actually, I'm thinking about staying."

Something flared deep inside him, a small spark of hope, quickly doused by a wave of panic. "Staying?"

She nodded. "Someone's interested in buying the farm; I don't think I want to sell, but the estate can't be settled until I decide. I thought I needed to be here for awhile before making any decisions."

He fought down the riot of emotions hammering at his

29

chest. How much longer could he stand here, growing more and more lightheaded from the soft rose scent of her cologne, getting lost in those enormous, searching eyes?

"I, ah, I'm sorry I wasn't here . . . when your grandfather died." It had been nine years since he'd seen her. She had been in town two years ago, for her grandfather's funeral, but he'd been on vacation. Relief had mingled with disappointment when he returned and heard that he'd missed her.

"You were in Canada."

He shot her a surprised look.

"I asked around. I had hoped to see you."

He changed the subject. "It's taken all this time to find a buyer for the farm?" *How long could they volley this meaningless small talk back and forth without really saying anything?*

She shrugged. "It's a lot of land, a big risk the way things are for farmers these days."

He nodded in agreement, shifting from one foot to the other. "I, ah, should be going. I promised to show Dan and Jennifer around the campus," he said awkwardly, starting to move even as he spoke. "They're probably waiting for me." He hesitated. "Well—it's great seeing you again, Freddi."

"Mitch." Her voice was low but insistant.

He froze, dragging his gaze to her face.

"You're"—she glanced at his left hand, then met his eyes—"still single?"

Resentment welled up in him. He felt himself flush as he stared at her. "Yes." *Does that give you some twisted sense of satisfaction, Freddi?*

"So am I," she said softly.

Before he could think, he said, "I know." In spite of himself, he read her press regularly. There had been a man once, a brief engagement that apparently hadn't worked.

His eyes locked with hers and clung. After an awkward silence, she glanced away. "I thought maybe we could get together," she said quietly, "to catch up on one another."

Slowly, she looked back to him, waiting.

Angry with his own lack of composure, he forced a note of brightness into his voice. "Sure. I want to hear all about your life. It may be hard to find the time this week, though. There's a lot going on . . . ." Feeling clumsy and glaringly transparent, he let his voice trail off.

"What about after the musical tonight?"

"The musical? You're coming?"

"I thought I would." She smiled at him. "You're directing the concert choir, aren't you?"

He nodded stiffly as his mind sped forward, then lurched in reverse, scrambling for an excuse. "I—I'm not sure, Freddi." *Don't do it. . .you can't handle it . . .* "I have company for the week—the couple who were just here. They'll be going back to my place with me, after we rig a floodlight up at Abby's—"

"Abby?"

He sketchily explained about Abby, then the security light.

When she remained quiet, he looked away for an instant, then back to her. *Don't be a jerk. . .you don't have to do this, you're crazy to even consider it. . .you don't owe her anything.*

"I suppose. . .you could join us." *You clown. . .what, you're going to offer her homemade ice cream and cookies next? Maybe she'd like a piece of your heart, too. . . she took most of it with her nine years ago anyway, you might as well let her have the rest.*

She searched his eyes. "Really? I wouldn't be intruding?"

Yes, you'd be intruding. . .intruding on my hard-won peace, Freddi Leigh. . .an intrusion I can't afford. . .not again. . . . "No, not. . .at all. You could maybe, ah, sit with the others at the musical. If you want to, I mean," he added

31

hastily. At her quick nod of agreement, he hurried on. "That way we can all meet afterward and go to my place."

"I'd like that," she said without hesitating. "If you're sure your friends won't mind."

He tried to clear his throat, but managed only a choking sound. "I'm sure they won't."

"Good. Well, I suppose I should sign in, or whatever it is I'm supposed to do today. Could you show me where the registration office is?"

Eager to get out of range of those watchful, studying eyes, Mitch began to move as soon as she asked. "You need to go to the lobby in the Student Center. That's where I was headed."

As always, she walked as if she knew exactly where she was going and hadn't the slightest doubt that whatever she wanted would be waiting for her when she arrived.

"Where are you staying?" he asked as they started toward the entrance.

"I'd planned to stay at the farm, but it'll be another day or two before Mrs. Kraker gets the house aired out and the kitchen stocked for me. I'm at the Lodge for now." She smiled at him, and the ache began all over again.

The Lodge. He'd worked there all the way through high school. Bits and pieces of memories began to unroll, whipping through his mind with incredible speed and clarity, turning his emotions into a heated feud of bittersweet contradictions.

A little-girl Freddi tugging at his hand just inside the park entrance to Briar Rose Glen, her thin face flushed with awe at the sight of a doe and its fawn poised in the twilight shadows. . . . A thirteen-year-old Freddi beside him on a scented summer morning, walking him to work as she trotted along on her way to a tennis lesson, her sunburned nose beginning to peel, her baseball cap tilted back over her pony tail. . . . A teenage Freddi, leaning contentedly against his shoulder as

32

they watched the sun fold itself up and slip lazily down behind Vision Lake on a warm, sultry August evening. . . . A grown-up Freddi pressing her face against his shoulder the night before she left for Ohio State. . . .

"I have to try, Mitch. . .if I stay here, I'll never know whether I could have made it or not. . .at least understand why I have to try. . . . I'll come back to you, Mitch, I promise you, I'll come back."

It was nine years later; she had come back.

She watched him out of the corner of her eye as they approached the front doors of the Center, still somewhat dazed by how different he was—and yet so much the same.

More than a boy all those years ago, yet not quite a man, she had often caught pieces of a vision, fleeting glimpses of what he promised to be. . .someday.

Now it was someday. And he was more, much more than she'd ever anticipated.

The wiry, always too-thin boy with the big, sad eyes and the uncertain, vulnerable smile was no longer too thin, no longer a boy. He moved with the slender, confident grace of a man who knew himself—who he was, what he was doing, where he was going—and was comfortable with what he knew. The light spray of freckles across the bridge of his nose was nearly obscured by the bronze of his skin, and the deep dimple in the middle of his chin was hidden by a dark, closely trimmed beard. His hair, still thick and springy, was a little longer but not quite so curly as she remembered. And although he was still lean and lanky—she'd often teased him that he looked like a hungry cowboy—his shoulders were now wider, his jaw stronger, and he no longer looked hungry.

But the eyes . . . the eyes were still sad, and the smile was still vulnerable.

33

He was still Mitch. Mitch, who could stab her heart and shatter her defenses with one tender look, one soft word of affection, one gentle touch of caring.

Instinctively, she tried to raise a protective wall between her emotions and his profile, then remembered that she was done with walls.

"So—tell me about your friends," she said, more in an attempt to get him to look at her again than to make conversation.

"Dan and Jennifer?" He nodded but kept his gaze straight ahead. "They're pretty special."

"Was that a guide dog with them?"

"Yes. Dan's been blind for over six years." As if anticipating her question, he explained, "It was a car accident. The other driver was drunk."

She grimaced, saying nothing for a few seconds. "What does he do? Is he one of the faculty?"

"No, they're here to lead a workshop. Dan owns a Christian radio station in West Virginia. And writes music— good music."

His smile brightened a little and now he *did* look at her. "Do you remember anything about the '72 Olympics? You would have been, what, about eleven? I was probably a freshman."

She thought for a moment. "Not much. Why?"

"There was an American swimmer from West Virginia who won two or three gold medals. They called him the 'Swimming Machine'."

She looked at him, still not sure what he was getting at. "That rings a bell. I did some research on the Munich Olympics for a book a few years ago."

"That was Dan," Mitch said, opening one of the double doors to the Center and waiting for her to step through. "Daniel Kaine."

She stopped halfway through the door. "Really?" A piece

34

of a memory appeared, a photo of a young giant's flushed, happy face, his eyes clouded with tears as the gold medal was slipped over his head.

"How does a man like that cope with being blind?" she questioned, walking into the lobby.

"Extremely well, as a matter of fact," Mitch said. "He has an awesome faith."

"I should think he'd need every ounce of it."

There were only a few people inside the cinnamon-and-beige lobby, most of them thinly scattered around the lounge area off to the right. They stood looking at each other for a moment. She thought Mitch seemed slightly less awkward now. Still uncomfortable, but at least his eyes had lost that wild, desperate glint that made her feel he wanted nothing more than to bolt and run from her.

His gaze on her was openly questioning, as if he were looking for answers, probing her thoughts. It hurt to see the doubt, the uncertainty in those eyes that had once looked at her with only warmth and affection and caring.

"You'll need to go down there," he finally said, pointing to a table at the other end of the long, narrow hall. "The lady in the pink and white blouse should have everything you need."

She glanced in the direction of his gesture. Turning back to him, she said, "I'll see you later tonight, then?"

He gave a small nod, seeming eager to get away. "I'll look you up before the music starts. Come a little early, if you can, so you can meet Dan and Jennifer—and Abby." He walked away from her, moving as if he could barely restrain himself from running.

Unable to look away from him until he turned the corner and disappeared, Freddi drew the first deep breath she'd been able to catch since seeing him in the parking lot.

Her heart had soared at the sight of him, only to plummet at the bitterness and hurt she'd encountered the moment they faced one another. At least, he wasn't married. The relief she'd felt upon learning that he was still single had made her want to weep.

Married or not, the past is dead. . . .He's a man you haven't seen for years, not the boy who would have died for you. . .that was yesterday.

But she had held on to enough of yesterday to give her hope. And it was that hope that had brought her home.

Mitch was still Mitch, boy-become-man, the same Mitch who had once known her better than anyone else had ever known her. . .the Mitch who had grown up protecting her, defending her. . .loving her. . . .

She glanced around the half-empty hallway. This was Mitch's place, his dream—the dream he'd found in the very surroundings she had been so eager to leave.

Now she was back, searching for whatever might be left of that long ago dream of her own. Because at some point during the longest hour of one seemingly endless night, she had finally realized that the reason her own dream had continued to elude her, to slip always just beyond her grasp, was that she had left it here—right here in Derry Ridge.

Somewhere in this town, on this mountain, in the searching, accusing eyes of the man who had just left her, was whatever might remain of that dream. She had to find out if there was still enough left to build on.

She had made a number of new beginnings over the past few months. This one, she knew, would be the most difficult of all.

3

The evening was deceptively tranquil, a peaceful pool contradicting the maelstrom of Freddi's emotions.

Sweet and warm, the summer-like breeze was faintly scented with wildflowers and anticipation. The gentle, lulling sound of the nearby Derry River could be heard during the few seconds of silence preceding the musical's finale, and lanterns bathed the descending twilight with flickering gold.

Hundreds of people were gathered on the lawn. Some had brought their own chairs; others shared blankets on the ground. After coaxing both Daniel and Jennifer to sing with the choir, Mitch had set up chairs for Abby and Freddi near the wooden platform erected for the choir.

Freddi liked the Kaines, had immediately warmed to the vivacious, dark-eyed Jennifer with her unassuming friendliness and the tall, powerful-looking Daniel with his gentle smile and hearty laugh. She particularly appreciated the way both of them had displayed, after the first few awkward moments of introduction, more interest in her as a person than as a public figure. It was an attitude she encountered too rarely.

Once the performance had begun, Freddi found it unsettling, even disturbing to watch Mitch. With consummate skill and sensitivity, he brought forth a rich, triumphant offering of music that soared above the campus lawn and out across the valley. Several times she had to fight back tears at the remembrance of things past. . .and things lost.

In the instant's hush preparatory to the final number, Freddi allowed her attention to wander for the first time in nearly an hour. Something off in the distance to her left caught her attention, and she straightened a little in the lawn chair to get a better look.

The man would have been impossible to miss. A huge, towering column in black apparel, he stood on an incline that flanked the left side of the chapel, several yards away from the outside fringe of the crowd.

The word *sinister* flashed through Freddi's mind as she studied him. He was immense, several inches over six feet, with the massive, heavily muscled frame of a professional body builder. His skin was remarkably white, nearly as white as his hair, of which only a military-short burr was visible around the sides of a black shooter's cap. Even his enormous arms, only partially exposed in the short-sleeved black shirt, were surprisingly fair.

She couldn't see his eyes; in spite of the fact that dusk was rapidly settling over the mountain, he wore a pair of dark aviator glasses. An involuntary shiver snaked along the back of Freddi's neck as she wondered about the eyes behind the glasses. She had the unnerving sensation that they were carefully and deliberately scrutinizing every face in the crowd, studying them, committing them to memory.

Freddi had spent too many years gathering research in police stations and courtrooms not to react to such a blatantly suspicious-looking figure. Her eyes narrowed in speculation as she continued to study his hulking frame. Instinct told her he was probably an albino, and the same instinct suggested that he was most likely carrying a gun, although none was visible.

Carefully, she unzipped the side pouch of her handbag and withdrew a slimline camera no larger than a compact. Palming it, she lifted her hand to her face as if to glance in a mirror, then smoothly released the shutter. Dropping the camera back inside her purse, she returned her attention to the choir, whose voices were now climbing toward the majestic climax of the musical.

During the almost deafening ovation that greeted the finale, Freddi glanced once more to the gentle swell of ground beside the chapel. The man was gone, but a lingering uneasiness chilled her as she stared into the thickening shadows cloaking the campus.

The atmosphere in Mitch's living room later that night was, at best, tense. With a pang of sympathy for him, Jennifer noted the tightness around Mitch's eyes, the slight trembling of his hands every time his gaze encountered Freddi's. He seemed almost bewildered, she thought, as if he knew he had a hopelessly awkward situation on his hands for which there was no readily accessible solution.

Ever since their arrival at the cabin over an hour ago, he'd been trying a little too hard to be carefully polite to Freddi. In turn, she met his guarded courtesy with what appeared to be a combination of restrained affection and growing disappointment.

The problem seemed to be, Jennifer noted with rising interest, that neither Freddi nor Mitch could keep their eyes off one another for more than a moment or two. Every look that passed between them crackled with tension. Every word exchanged seemed laced with hidden meaning.

There had been a comfortable amount of laughter and good-natured teasing while they were setting up the floodlight at Abby's cabin, but now a blanket of constraint had fallen over the room. The laughter seemed forced, the conversation stiff.

It was Abby who unknowingly honed the tension of the evening to its peak. By ten o'clock they had consumed nearly two dozen cookies and a pot of coffee. Jennifer was sitting next to Daniel on the enormous black-and-white sofa that rimmed one entire wall of the living room, while Mitch stood in front of the wide stone fireplace facing them. Freddi had settled herself into a massive leather easy chair, her feet tucked snugly beneath her; she looked comfortably—though deceptively, Jennifer suspected—at ease with her surroundings.

Abby was just returning from the kitchen with a fresh pot of coffee when she came to an abrupt stop only inches away from Freddi, staring at her with wide, excited eyes. Jennifer had noticed the older woman studying Freddi throughout the evening, but she was caught completely off guard by what came next.

With the coffee pot extended outward, the bright-eyed Abby exclaimed, "You're the girl in the picture!"

Freddi gave Abby a puzzled look. "The girl in the picture?"

With an eager nod, Abby transferred her attention to a flushed Mitch. "The picture in your wallet, Mitch! Remember, you let me look at the snapshots once, and I asked you about the girl with the long black hair?"

Turning back to Freddi, she continued to gape at her. "But you're much prettier now, dear. You were just a little girl in the picture." Almost as an afterthought, she added, "Mitch said the two of you used to be best friends."

As Jennifer watched, Freddi slowly turned to Mitch with a look that was both pleased and questioning. "Yes. We were."

Mitch, who seemed to have developed an acute interest in something on the floor beside his foot, said nothing.

As if to rescue him from his embarrassment, Freddi moved casually to a different subject. "Mitch, is there someone around town these days who looks like he might have OD'd on steroids?"

Mitch's head came up with an unmistakable look of relief. "What?"

Freddi shrugged. "I saw him tonight during the performance. Monster of a guy—six-six or more. Arms like hams, legs like tree trunks. He was wearing some kind of a black outfit that looked almost like a uniform. And sunglasses," she added, lifting a cynical brow, "though the sun was long gone."

Mitch frowned and shook his head. "Where did you see him?"

"He was standing at the edge of the lawn near the chapel, just up from the river."

Again Mitch shook his head. "I don't think so. Abby, did you see him?"

"Hm?" Obviously, Abby wasn't listening. She had plopped down on a small rocking chair across from Mitch and was playing with Pork Chop, a spotted cocker spaniel—one of several dogs that seemed to parade at will in and out of Mitch's cabin.

When Mitch repeated his question, adding Freddi's details, Jennifer was puzzled by Abby's unexpected reaction. Her face paled to a waxen sheen, and her voice had a dreamlike quality as she asked, "A big man in black clothes? With sunglasses?"

"Did you see him, Abby?" Mitch prompted.

She didn't answer. Instead, perched on the edge of the chair, she began to hug herself, rocking forward and back as she stared out the glass doors into the darkness.

Glancing from Abby to the door, Mitch stepped away from the fireplace and went to her. "Abby," he said softly.

Slowly, she turned to look up at him, saying nothing. Her expression had cleared somewhat, but her eyes were still troubled, her body rigid.

Mitch dropped down to a stoop in front of her. His voice was gentle as he reached for her hand. "Abby, is something wrong? Something about the man Freddi saw?"

"Man?" Her gaze was vacant now. Even the glint of anxiety had faded. "What man, dear?"

Mitch studied her with concern for a long moment, then

41

seemed to relax. Watching him, Jennifer sensed that this wasn't the first time he'd been through this with Abby.

He stood and, glancing at his watch, said, "We'd better get you home, sweetheart. It's getting late." Taking both of Abby's hands, he helped her up from the chair. With an uncertain look, he then turned to Freddi. "I'll take you back to your car after we drop Abby at her place. All right?"

Freddi merely nodded, and, uncoiling herself from the chair, slowly got to her feet.

The silence in the cabin after they'd gone was unsettling. Daniel broke it by bending forward and fumbling hopefully around the cookie platter. "Anything left?"

"Here." Jennifer guided his hand to one of two remaining brownies.

"Is this the last one? I'll share."

Distracted, Jennifer said, "No, it's all yours."

"You're bothered about Abby, aren't you?" he asked with his usual perception.

"That was strange, wasn't it? She seemed so—distant. I had the distinct feeling that she didn't even know where she was for a moment."

Finishing off the brownie, Daniel wiped his hands on a napkin and sank back against the couch again. "Tell me about Abby."

She looked at him. "She's plump. And pretty. She has these incredibly big blue eyes—china doll eyes. I imagine she's somewhere in her mid-sixties."

"And she troubles you."

Jennifer thought for a moment. "It's as if there's something. . .missing about her. She's warm and sweet and delightful. . . ." Uncertainly, she let her words trail off.

"But?" he interrupted, waiting.

She glanced away, staring into the cold fireplace. What *did* trouble her about Abby? For a moment tonight she'd half-expected her to rise from her chair and go walking outside, into the darkness.

There had been an instant when Abby had seemed to take on a kind of strange awareness, to teeter on the very edge of some sort of recognition. But the moment had fled too quickly for Jennifer to be certain she hadn't simply imagined it.

With a sigh, she turned back to Daniel. "I'm not sure," she said vaguely.

He patted the cushion beside him, and she moved closer. Pulling her into the circle of his arm, he coaxed her head against his shoulder. At the same time, he lowered his free hand over the other side of the couch to stroke the ears of a dozing Sunny, who had become a pillow for Mitch's little cocker spaniel.

"So how does it feel to have spent an evening with a celebrity?" he asked, lightly resting his chin on top of her head.

"Freddi? Actually, it's hard to remember who she is—that she's famous, I mean. She's incredibly easy to be with, not at all what I would have expected."

"Am I right in thinking that Mitch doesn't find it quite that easy to be with her?" he asked.

Again she sighed. "Poor Mitch."

"Poor Mitch?"

"I think his life is about to become extremely complicated."

"Ah." He nodded wisely. "The lady Gwynevere, I presume?"

"There's a story there." Jennifer had always loved a good mystery. And a good mystery seasoned with a touch of romance, as seemed to be the case with this particular situation, was a combination that never failed to ram her curiosity into overdrive.

"Oh, a *story*." Daniel grinned in anticipation.

"Exactly. You should see the way she looks at him."

43

"Something like the way you look at me?"

She tilted her head to glance up at him. "Well . . . yes, as a matter of fact."

"And Mitch?"

"Mitch," she replied after only a second's hesitation, "looks at *her* like a man standing on the edge of a cliff trying to decide whether he should take a flying leap or turn and run."

"I can identify with that. That's pretty much how I felt when I realized I was falling in love with you."

A thought struck her, and she narrowed her eyes to study his face. "And just how is it that you *know* the way I look at you?"

She thought his smile might be a little smug when he said, "Oh, I've been told."

"Gabe-the-Mouth strikes again," she said knowingly.

He shrugged off the reference to his brother-in-law and best friend. "No shame in a woman showing her love for her husband."

She grinned at him, waiting.

One heavy dark brow lifted in anticipation. "Don't you agree?"

"Oh, I do."

"So?"

Agreeably, she wrapped her arms around his neck.

4

Squeezed snugly between Abby and Mitch in the front seat of his blue pickup, Freddi tried not to think about Mitch's closeness. She defended her unsettled feelings by reminding herself that almost a decade had passed since the two of them had bumped along a deserted mountain road. It was difficult to realize that the tall, confident man behind the steering wheel was really Mitch, that she was home, and that they were together again.

No. Not *together*. Too many years of separation lay between them, too many years of differences and distance for her to pretend this was the same Mitch she'd left behind or that anything was even remotely the same as it once had been.

Nostalgia rushed at her, sharpened by the lonely silence of the night. A tidal wave of images threatened to break her heart. The shadowed silhouette of Mitch's profile beside her was all too well-remembered; the faint cinnamon-clove scent from the rock candy he still carried in his pocket was too achingly familiar.

She had been unable to stop a smile at the sight of his sporty blue truck. There had been a time—so many years ago it now seemed like forever—when she had sat on a river bank holding hands with a lean-faced boy, listening as he solemnly declared, "Someday, I'm going to buy me a bright blue truck with a shine you can see your pretty face in, instead of driving you around in an ugly old broken-down wagon truck."

Mitch's dreams had always been incredibly simple, as uncomplicated as the boy he'd been, as gentle as the man he seemed to have become. Back then her own dreams had seemed so vastly more important, so much bigger and brighter. . . .

The drive to find out what lay beyond Derry Ridge had been at the heart of all her dreams for as long as she could remember. She had entertained only one other ambition throughout all the years of growing up: to write, and to write so well that all the world would rush to read what she had written.

Although he'd pretended to understand the fury that drove her, Mitch had never really been able to comprehend her desire to reach beyond what she already had. He had always loved the Ridge and everything it encompassed: its people, its music, its entire history and cultural heritage. While he had yearned to dig in and become one with the mountain, Freddi had longed to explore the other side.

For as long as she could remember, Mitch had ached to have a place of his own, a "homeplace" right here on the Ridge. And in spite of his inability—or his refusal, as she had thought of it then—to comprehend *her* need to get away, she thought she had instinctively understood *his* need to stay.

His father had deserted his teenage wife not long after Mitch was born. Before Mitch was old enough to go to school, his mother dumped him on a relative and headed for her own "fresh start" somewhere in North Carolina, leaving Mitch to spend the rest of his childhood being flung from one indifferent aunt or uncle to another. He had never known the security, the stability of a real home.

In contrast, Freddi had grown up under the shelter of a widowed, doting grandfather after the death of her parents in an airline crash. Her father, the community's only veterinarian, and her mother, a Latin teacher at the high school, had left Freddi financially independent. She had marched confidently through childhood and adolescence, much

46

loved and admittedly much too pampered by her grandfather.

It was no wonder she and Mitch had reached for different stars. She was glad to see that he had finally attained his dreams, or was at least well on his way to doing so. He deserved it all—the directorship of the new Heritage department, the doctorate he'd recently completed, and the credit for a newly published textbook on eastern Kentucky folk music which he'd co-authored with another instructor on campus. Along the way he had built not only the cabin home he'd long planned but a meaningful campus ministry as well.

Oh, Lord, why couldn't I have realized then how very small those tinsel dreams of mine were? How empty, how temporary, how deceitful. . . .

Beside her, Abby spoke, rousing Freddi from her memories. "The mountain's nice at night, isn't it? So restful and quiet and untroubled."

Freddi smiled at the older woman in the darkness. "You like it here very much, don't you, Abby?"

"Oh my, I certainly do! You'll come in and see my place, won't you?" she urged Freddi. "You can meet Peaches, too."

"Peaches?"

"Peaches," Mitch explained dryly, "is a mountain lion posing as a cat. She has teeth like a chain saw and claws like carpet tacks. Believe me," he said with a wry twist of his mouth, "her name is the only sweet thing about the little monster."

"Oh, Mitch, she's only a kitten!" Abby insisted heatedly. "She just likes to roughhouse with you."

"She likes to make me bleed, you mean." He gave Freddi a conspiratorial wink, another familiar leftover from yesterday that made her heart skip.

The three of them sat in silence the rest of the way up the

47

road. Both windows were down, and the night breeze, a little cooler now, felt good on Freddi's face.

The strong scent of pine and hardwood meshed with the heady odor of rich, spring-warmed earth and endless varieties of mountain wildflowers. Somewhere on the hillside a dog howled. Freddi shivered as if she'd heard a sound of mourning. This late at night, the Ridge was a lonesome place to be, at times forbidding in its isolated darkness.

As Mitch pulled into the gravel turnaround at Abby's cabin, Freddi suddenly realized that it was *too* dark.

"I thought you set the floodlight to turn on at nine," she said.

Mitch glanced at her, then the cabin. "I did. The timer must not have worked."

Freddi sat forward. Draped by the shroud of darkness, the cabin was almost indistinguishable.

Something didn't seem quite right. But what?

The door.

"Mitch—" Keeping her eyes straight ahead, she put a hand on his arm.

Letting the engine idle, he shot a questioning look at her, then at the darkened cabin. The sky that had been clear a short time before was now thick with clouds, the thin slice of moon blotted into oblivion.

His eyes still on the cabin, Mitch reached over to add the pickup's overhead running lights to the headlight beams. In the tumbling roll of light that hit the front porch, the open doorway gaped like a black hole in a garishly lighted carnival house.

Abby gasped and started to open the truck door.

"Wait!" Mitch flung his arm out to stop her.

His gaze swept their surroundings as, leaning across both Freddi and Abby, he pushed the door lock down, then rolled up the window.

Straightening, he rolled up the window on his side before

48

opening the glove compartment. Withdrawing a large crescent wrench, he smacked it once lightly against the palm of his hand.

Abby looked blankly from the wrench to his face. "What's that for, Mitch? What are you going to do?"

He didn't answer as he sat, unmoving, scanning the cabin and the dark, forest-covered hillside looming behind it.

After a long moment, he quietly unlocked his door. "Stay here," he ordered in a harsh whisper. "Keep the doors locked. If you need me, lean on the horn."

He put his hand on the door handle, but Freddi caught his arm. "I'll go with you."

"No!" He whipped around in the seat, repeating in a lower voice, "No. Let me take a look first. Just stay put until I come back."

He opened the door slowly, grimacing at the metal's loud, grating squeak of protest.

Freddi snapped the lock down as soon as he leaped from the truck, then watched him take the flagstone walk in quick, cautious steps. The tense silence inside the truck was broken only by her own shallow breathing and the sound of Abby pulling worriedly at the knuckles on her hands.

All the way up the walk, Mitch told himself this was probably the work of the same gang of unruly teens that had been vandalizing various businesses and residences throughout the county over the past few months. Their random mischief had been witnessed on a number of occasions, but they were still freely roaming about the Ridge. Undoubtedly, this was the same bunch responsible for shooting out the security light the night before.

At the porch, he glanced around, seeing nothing. Quietly, he stepped up onto the wide-planked floor and crossed to the open door.

He stopped, pressing himself against the porch wall. After

a moment he looked in. The wrench felt heavy in his hand, and he tightened his grip on it.

Using his foot, he pushed the door open a little farther and took one cautious step over the threshold.

The blackness of the room stopped him. His heart pounded as he fumbled for the light switch on the wall beside the door.

Reassured by the immediate wash of light that sprayed the room when he flipped the switch, he stepped the rest of the way inside.

His first sensation was that of violence.

The light that usually appeared warm and golden now seemed stark and cruel as it revealed the cabin's defilement in ugly detail.

The seat of the couch had been slashed all the way across, its ruffled cushions tossed to the floor. Books had been spilled from the shelves beside the fireplace, some ripped from their bindings and pitched across the room. The single drawer of the petite spinet desk he'd given Abby for Christmas was overturned on the floor, its contents strewn haphazardly nearby. In front of the window and beside the end table were shattered pieces of broken lamps.

In spite of the cool breeze blowing in through the open door, Mitch's face grew hot, seared by angry disbelief.

He took a couple of unsteady steps toward the middle of the room, his mind struggling to comprehend the destruction.

Why? What drove a bunch of kids to this kind of wanton savagery?

His heart pounding, he left the room and started down the hallway toward the kitchen. He held his breath in dread as he flipped on the overhead light.

Dishes and crockery lay shattered on the handwoven rug, and half-empty cupboards gaped, their contents tossed onto the pine counter or on the floor.

Mitch felt sick, not only because of the mindless, obscene violation, but because a chilling whisper at the back of his mind teased that he hadn't yet seen the worst.

A frantic inner voice told him to run, to get out.

What, and bring Abby inside to face this, without knowing what else was in store?

His legs shaking with the effort, he climbed over the rubble on the floor and started for the bedroom.

Feeling his way through the darkness to the bedside table, he found the lamp intact and turned it on.

He could have wept at what they'd done in here; he did moan aloud. His pulse hammered painfully in his ears, and he choked against the dryness of his throat. He caught his breath, willing his head to clear as he fought for control.

The newly stained louvered doors of the closet had been ripped from their hinges; Abby's sparse wardrobe had been flung to the floor. The drawers of her small bureau had been ripped free and overturned, their contents tossed helter-skelter around the room.

The gold and ginger room that always made him think of a field of sunflowers now appeared forlorn and pathetic in its desecration.

He took a step backward, turned to leave the room, then froze.

Peaches.

Where was the cat?

Outside, he realized with relief. The door had been open, hadn't it? The cat had most likely dashed from the house at the first sign of the intruders.

Just to be sure, he ducked across the hall, into the small bath that opened off the bedroom.

Everything was normal, except for the shelves of the tall, narrow linen closet. Towels and sheets lay scattered on the floor, but otherwise nothing seemed to have been touched.

As he returned to the kitchen, a hard, grating anger edged its way past the shock and began to take control of his emotions. This was more than vandalism, more than teenage mischief. Abby had been violated, robbed of her privacy, her security, her safety. In Mitch's mind, this was almost as bad as an outright attack on her person.

What if she had been here?

He shook off the question. Obviously, it wouldn't have happened if she'd been here. These kids preyed on empty houses and vacant cars. They weren't interested in a confrontation with a property owner.

He realized heavily that she was going to have to see what had been done in here, and the thought of her vulnerable face when she viewed the destruction made him ill.

He became aware that he was still clinging to the wrench in his hand. He pocketed it, then crossed the kitchen to the broom closet. Apparently, it had escaped their notice, since the curtained opening was still closed.

Brushing the calico material to one side, he reached for the broom, his eyes searching the darkness for the dustpan Abby kept in the corner.

The sound of his voice when he cried out so stunned him that he jumped back, losing his balance. Lurching to right himself, he swayed, slapped the wall with his hand and waited.

He could hear the thunder of his own heart, felt the cold trickle of perspiration track the nape of his neck as he again pulled back the curtain.

As he let the image register, bile swelled in his throat, sour enough to choke him. His stomach heaved, and a black wave rolled over him with dizzying force.

It was Peaches. The head of the small, spotted kitten hung at a crooked angle. She was dead, her neck obviously broken.

Fighting nausea, struggling to breathe, Mitch dropped

down and stared in horror at the lifeless cat. He touched her once, his fingers trembling and his eyes tearing as he remembered the times he'd teased Abby about her harmless little pet.

Glancing at the shelf just above his head, he reached for an old towel and gently laid it over the kitten.

Hauling himself up, he reeled at the movement and gripped the corner of the wall until his head cleared.

He had to think. He couldn't let Abby see the cat. His eyes swept the room as he fought to bring his mind into focus. Rage battered at him, followed by a stirring of fear.

He raked a hand across the back of his neck, felt it clammy with cold perspiration. *How could he tell Abby?*

He flinched, jolted by the remembrance that both she and Freddi were still outside in the truck. Turning, he fled the kitchen and started down the hall toward the front door.

Both of them were standing just inside the open doorway, staring at him, Freddi with angry disbelief, Abby with the stunned gaze of a wounded animal. "We were afraid something had happened to you...." Freddi's voice caught, then died away at the scene in front of her.

Raising a hand to stop them from coming the rest of the way in, Mitch quickly crossed the room.

The look on Abby's face was as terrible as he'd known it would be. Her incredulous blue eyes, glistening with unshed tears, slowly scanned the destruction of the room, then turned a look of pleading denial on Mitch.

His mind fumbled for words, groped for an answer to the unspoken question in her gaze. But the best he could do was to put a steadying arm around her. When he felt her begin to quake beneath his touch, he tightened his clasp on her shoulder.

"Mitch?" Abby's voice caught on his name as she lifted her eyes to his.

There was nothing he could say to her, nothing he could do

for her. The only thing now was to get her out of the cabin.

With a firm hand, he began to turn her toward the door, but she stood frozen.

"Abby—you mustn't come in. Come on, let's go back to the truck." Again he tried to turn her away from the room.

"But, Mitch, what . . ."

"Abby, please—"

"Who—" Her voice broke. "*Why, Mitch?*"

Glancing over her head, he caught Freddi's gaze and silently urged her to help him.

She moved to take Abby's other arm, and the two of them managed to lead her out to the porch.

At the back of his mind, a warning sounded, chilling Mitch with the thought that whoever did this could easily be close-by, watching from the woods, waiting.

His pulse hammering, he scanned the thick, inky darkness surrounding them as they started down the porch steps. His hand went to the wrench in his back pocket in a gesture of reassurance.

Abruptly, Abby stopped and tried to pull away. "Peaches! I can't leave without Peaches, Mitch—she'll be terrified—"

Mitch shot an agonizing look at Freddi. With a grim nod of understanding, she tightened her hold on Abby's arm. "Abby, Mitch will take care of Peaches. Let's you and I go to the truck," she urged with firm kindness.

Only when the three of them were safely locked inside the pickup, this time with Abby in the middle, did he tell her, as gently as possible, what had happened to Peaches.

5

The rain began the next morning. Its beginning was true to form for a Kentucky mountain rainstorm—deceptively mild and teasingly insignificant. As a native, Freddi knew it was only a matter of hours before the drizzle would become a downpour.

Not that the gloomy weather was all bad. Seated next to a window in the dining room of the Lodge, she studied the pewter-misted morning with the thought that an anticipated rainstorm should provide a safe enough topic of conversation for her and Mitch when he arrived for breakfast.

If he arrived. Suggesting that they meet for breakfast this morning had been strictly an act of impulse, and Mitch's awkward hesitation had been almost painfully obvious. Still, it had been his idea to strand her at the Lodge without a car.

He'd caught her completely off guard the night before with his insistence that she leave her car in the campus parking lot and let him drive her to the Lodge. When she protested, reminding him that she needed a way in to her morning workshop, Mitch had hesitated only a moment before saying, "That's no problem. I'm going to Abby's place first thing in the morning to ... take care of the cat. I'll drive on up to the Lodge afterward and you can ride in with me."

When she would have objected, he silenced her with a flat, obstinate, "You've got no business driving that road by yourself this late. Especially after what happened at Abby's."

It *had* been late—nearly two—when they'd finally got Abby settled in at Mitch's cabin. Daniel, with a quiet, soothing kindness that belied his somewhat intimidating size and powerfully built frame, and Jennifer, with her brisk, no-

55

nonsense manner that seemed to balance her apparent mother-hen instincts, had both been wonderfully helpful with the distraught Abby.

For her own part, Freddi had been restless throughout the night. The hours she hadn't spent sparring with herself about her feelings for Mitch had been spent replaying in vivid detail the destruction at Abby's cabin. Force of habit had stirred numerous nagging questions about Abby.

The woman intrigued her: her missing past, her lack of identity, the circumstances that had brought her to Derry Ridge. Freddi's mystery-writer mind refused to take a passive role when presented with a puzzle such as this.

The unanswered questions surrounding the winsome Abby were too many—and too arresting—to simply disregard. Nor had she managed to shake the downright creepy image of that black-garbed behemoth standing on the campus green the night before. Odder still, by the time the first gray light of morning had begun to filter through her window, a core of suspicion had cemented itself firmly in her mind: there was a connection between the Monster Man and Abby. Freddi had learned to trust her hunches, and she wasn't at all sure it was mere coincidence that just when. . .

She was yanked abruptly out of her speculative brooding when the double doors to the dining room swung open and Mitch walked in. Opposing forces of longing and regret charged across the field of her emotions at the sight of him. Swallowing, she pulled in a steadying breath as she watched him cross the room in her direction.

He was wearing a yellow windbreaker, open over a white cotton sweater and pleated canvas pants. The rain had tightened the curl of his hair slightly, and his dark brows were knit together in a frown that clearly said he didn't consider this a smart idea. Not at all.

When he came to stand in front of her, he managed a brief, unconvincing smile. Glancing at her half-empty coffee cup, he asked, "Have you already eaten?" Freddi thought he sounded hopeful.

"No. I was waiting for you."

After a slight hesitation, he shrugged out of his windbreaker and hung it over the back of a chair, then sat down across from her.

"You look tired," she said. He looked more than tired. His eyes were smudged with deep shadows that hadn't been there the day before, and there was a tight, haggard look about him that left little doubt as to how short his night had been.

His eyebrows lifted meaningfully as he shrugged and picked up a menu.

"How's Abby this morning?"

He lay the menu on the table, then pushed it aside. "Confused. Hurt. Pretty much as you'd expect. She went to work, though."

It went on that way for several minutes. As if by agreement, they limited their conversation to the neutral subjects of Abby, the weather, and the view from the Lodge dining room. In between ordering breakfast and a few idle remarks about the food when it arrived, they exchanged awkward looks and wobbly smiles.

If their fingers accidentally brushed while reaching for the cream pitcher, Mitch flinched as if he'd been seared by an open flame. If their casual reminiscing happened to skirt too close to a shared memory, he simply blinked and quickly turned away.

"Have you talked to the police yet, about last night?" she asked, trying to keep the conversation as safely impersonal as he seemed to want it.

He scowled. "For all the good it did. Will Bannon is still chief," he said pointedly.

Freddi made a face at the memory of Derry Ridge's Chief of Police. Bannon had been pushing three hundred pounds and threatening an early retirement for as long as she could remember. His laziness was legend, surpassed only by his bigotry and savage contempt for "strangers." He would be hopelessly callous toward Abby's plight.

"He calls her the 'dipsy bag lady on the hill', if that tells you anything," Mitch added resentfully, finishing off his last bite of toast.

"He always was a compassionate soul." Freddi took a sip of coffee. Nibbling indifferently at her sweet roll, she said, "It's going to take some work, putting Abby's cabin in order. I'd like to help."

Mitch gave her a long, unreadable look before glancing down at his cup. "That's nice of you, but I think I can find some students willing to help later on this morning. I want to get it cleaned up as quickly as possible."

He filled both their cups from the stoneware coffee pot, then signaled their waitress to bring them more cream. After the girl had again retreated, he leaned forward, locking his fingers together on top of the table.

"I just wish there was a way to put those punks out of business," he said bitterly, staring at his hands.

"Mitch, do you really believe that what happened at Abby's place was vandalism?"

He looked up. "What else?"

She hesitated. "I think it might have been. . .something more."

Saying nothing, he frowned and waited.

"It seems to me that whoever tore Abby's cabin apart was looking for something."

Openly skeptical as well as puzzled, Mitch drew back a little in his chair, crossing his arms over his chest. "Looking for something? Like what?"

Running the tip of one finger around the rim of her coffee cup, Freddi took her time in answering. "Most of the damage done was methodical," she explained. "Oh, there was a certain amount of rage, violence—certainly killing the cat was senselessly sadistic. But the way the couch was ripped open, the desk emptied, the closets rifled—" She shook her head, meeting his gaze. "Whoever did that was after something."

His eyes narrowed. "After *what?*"

She shrugged. "There's no way of knowing. Maybe he doesn't know either. Maybe he's just looking for—whatever he can find."

"*He?*" Mitch lifted one brow in a dubious look.

"Probably. Somehow I think it's only one person."

He stared at her for a long time, long enough that she grew uncomfortable under his scrutiny.

"I suppose it follows that a mystery writer is part detective, too." He made no effort to soften the scorn behind his words.

She met his sarcasm with a quiet reply. "No. But I *do* spend a good deal of time around crime scenes. And police stations and courtrooms."

He seemed to relax somewhat. "That makes sense. I suppose that's why your books always ring true."

She blinked in surprise. "You read my books?"

He shrugged. "Why wouldn't I?"

Returning her attention to the rim of her coffee cup, she answered softly, "I guess. . .I just didn't think you would."

He shifted in his chair, changing the subject. "Are you serious about what you said? You think someone deliberately trashed Abby's place because they were trying to find something?"

"Yes." She leaned forward a little, lifting her eyes to his. "Mitch, what exactly do you know about Abby? Anything more than what you told me yesterday?"

He moved to pour more coffee for both of them. "No. How could I, when she knows so little about herself?"

"What about her clothes?"

59

"Her clothes?"

"What was she wearing when she came here? What did she have with her?"

He thought for a moment. "Until we took up a collection and bought some stuff for her, she had only one dress. It was . . . blue, I think. Faded."

"That's all?"

"That was it, other than some toiletries. Why?"

Freddi met his question with another. "What about a purse?"

He gave a nod of acknowledgment. "She had a purse, but it was virtually empty. No wallet, no ID. Just a couple of small pieces of jewelry and some tissues. And an empty pillbox," he added.

Freddi mulled that over for another instant. "It doesn't fit."

"What doesn't fit?"

"That a woman like Abby would show up with no money, no clothes, no possessions—and no past."

"A woman like Abby?" His brows drew together in a questioning frown.

"Haven't you noticed a certain"—she reached for the word she wanted—"*dignity* about her? A kind of understated elegance?"

For a long moment he looked at her. Then a slow-dawning light of recognition rose in his eyes. "Yes," he said, nodding his head slowly. "I *have*. I would never have been able to put a name to it, but it's something about the way she sits, certain ways she holds her hands, even her head—"

"Class."

At his puzzled look, she repeated, "*Class*. Abby has class."

His smile was soft and faintly tender as he echoed the word. "Class. . .that's it. . .that fits her. Abby's. . .a lady."

"Exactly." Freddi's imagination began to roll. "So what's a

60

genuine-article lady doing on top of a Kentucky mountain without a nickel to her name or a scrap of memory about her past?"

When he didn't answer, she went on. "You said the local police tried to dig up some background on her. How much of an effort do you think they really made?"

He shrugged. "I don't have any idea. I suppose they did what they could."

Freddi lifted her cup and drained the rest of her coffee before saying, "I have a friend in Chicago—a PI, one of the best in the business—who would probably do some checking for us, if I asked him to."

She could almost hear the questions forming in his mind as he studied her.

"Boyfriend?" His tone was light, but his eyes were hard.

"*Friend*," she emphasized.

His gold-flecked eyes continued to probe hers for a moment. Then he shook his head. "I don't think so."

She hadn't expected that. "Why not?"

He looked away. "I'm not sure we have the right. It seems... almost like prying." His voice held a sharp edge when he turned back to her, saying, "Besides, there's no money to pay someone like that. Even I know private investigators don't come cheap."

"I told you he's a friend. There wouldn't be a fee."

"He must be a *good* friend."

Unless he'd changed a great deal, the pointed remark and accompanying borderline sneer represented all the nastiness of which Mitch was capable, so Freddi decided to ignore the dig. "Aren't you curious enough to want to try?"

Again he glanced away. "What if there's some kind of trouble in Abby's past—something she was running away from?"

"That's a possibility. But it's also possible that there are

61

people in her past, people who love her and are trying to find her. A husband, children—what about them?"

As she watched, his eyes closed for an instant, then opened. He said nothing.

"Mitch," she probed quietly, "are you afraid of what we might find out?"

He turned back to her but remained silent until he'd taken a long drink of coffee. "Maybe I am. I'd hate to see Abby hurt."

Freddi hadn't expected him to admit what came next. "Maybe I'm also a little afraid of losing her. She's become really important to me."

"That's not likely to happen. Abby loves you."

He smiled a little, and she saw a brief flash of the younger, roguish Mitch when he cracked, "Yeah, well, it takes a certain amount of maturity to appreciate my charm."

For a long time they both continued to stare outside, saying nothing as they watched the light, steady rain. Finally Mitch broke the silence. "Go ahead."

She turned to look at him. "What?"

"Go ahead and ask your. . .friend. . .to see what he can find out. I don't like it, but I suppose it's the right thing to do." He shot her a look. "But anything he turns up gets run by me before it gets to Abby."

Freddi nodded. "Of course."

After another brief silence, he sighed heavily. "I just wish I knew what to do with her now."

"What do you mean?"

"She can't stay alone. Not after what happened last night." Jabbing at the table with his thumb, he added, "Especially if you're right about it being deliberate."

Freddi wasn't sure what sparked the idea in her mind. She was as surprised as Mitch seemed to be at the words that came out of her mouth. "How do you think Abby would feel about a roommate for a few days?"

"A roommate?"

She nodded. "Me."

She thought he was going to choke on the cinnamon ball he'd just popped into his mouth. "*You?* Stay with Abby?"

"Why not?"

His face tightened. "What exactly are you up to, Freddi?" he demanded. "A new plot? You smell the makings of another bestseller, is that it?"

She bristled. "I'm not up to anything, Mitch. I'm trying to help. Is that so inconceivable?"

He leaned forward, his eyes glinting with challenge. "Abby lives in a three room cabin on the top side of a mountain—a mountain which, as I recall, you were never overly fond of. She doesn't own a hot tub; she doesn't even own a television set. Her idea of entertainment is crocheting afghans for one of the local nursing homes." He stopped, brought his face even closer to hers and added caustically, "Not exactly the lifestyle to which you've become accustomed, is it, Freddi?"

Their eyes locked and held. "What exactly do you know about my lifestyle, Mitch?" she countered evenly.

"Point taken. But you still haven't told me what you're up to."

His expression was more than skeptical. It was openly hostile.

"I told you, I'd planned to stay at the farm," she said evenly. "But it's going to be a few days before I can settle in." Now warming to her own idea, she pressed on. "If Abby would have me, it would give you a little peace of mind, wouldn't it? At least she wouldn't be alone."

"She doesn't have room."

"She has a couch."

"Not anymore," he reminded her almost viciously.

She thought for a moment, then nodded. "I'll replace the couch. It can be my way of paying my keep, for however long

I stay with her."

His eyes narrowed even more as he studied her with open mistrust. Then, slowly, he eased away, sinking back against the chair. "Freddi. . .why did you come back?"

Unprepared for his bluntness, Freddi at first attempted to skate around the truth with a weak laugh. "I thought you were the man with all the answers this week. I'm doing a creative writing workshop, remember?"

"I'm sure you get more than your share of workshop invitations," he said acidly, his eyes still hard. "Try again, Freddi."

Gripping the rim of her saucer between both hands, she groped for an answer that would be honest but not too revealing. "I'm not sure you'd believe me."

His look never wavered. "It might take some doing, but try me."

Freddi swallowed, then looked away. Staring into the leaden gloom of the morning, she knew with unshakable assurance that it was too soon to tell him. . .everything.

"I just realized that it was time to. . .make some changes in my life."

Uncertainly, she looked back at him. His gaze was relentless, raking her face with undisguised suspicion. "What kind of changes, Freddi?"

She tried a careless shrug, but it came off badly. "My life's become. . .too fast, Mitch. Too fast, too frantic—too much. Even my writing is out of control. I have to take some time for myself, do some thinking. Besides," she added quickly, before he could interrupt with another sarcastic jibe, "I was homesick. Believe it or not, I was homesick."

Homesick for my best friend. . .my hero. . .my love.

She watched him, anticipating more sarcasm. Anticipating anything but what came.

His eyes were still wary but no longer contemptuous as he leaned toward her and said in a quiet, even voice, "Freddi, are you in some kind of trouble?"

She stared at him blankly. "Trouble?"

Still searching her face with what appeared to be genuine, if guarded, concern, he pressed. "Do you need help?"

He hadn't believed her. He hadn't even *heard* her. She suddenly felt incredibly sad. Was she really that shallow, that untrustworthy in his eyes...in his memory? "No, Mitch," she said softly. "I'm not in any kind of trouble. I simply wanted to come home, that's all."

For a long time he sat silently studying her. When he finally spoke, his words lined her heart with sorrow. "Freddi, if the Ridge wasn't big enough for you when you were eighteen, it's surely not big enough for you now. Not after being where you've been, doing all you've done. Don't forget how desperate you were to get away from here."

"That was a long time ago, Mitch."

"Some things don't change. The Ridge hasn't changed, Freddi."

But I have, Mitch...I have. "I was counting on that," she said softly.

He leaned back, his shoulders sinking heavily against the back of the chair. "You're really serious."

"Yes."

"It won't work, Freddi," he said, shaking his head slowly. "You'll never stay."

It has to work, Mitch...the only part of me that's worth anything is somewhere back here, on this mountain...with you. . . .

He got to his feet so abruptly the chair collided with the wall. "We'd better go."

She stood, fumbling in her purse for a pen to sign the check.

She jumped when his hand covered hers just long enough to slide the check from between her fingers. "I'll get it," he said, holding her gaze. "We don't have to go dutch any more." For an instant the faint smile in his eyes was unguarded and almost warm.

He took her arm as they started toward the cashier's counter. "There's a chapel service each morning at nine-fifteen," he said. "You'll have a few minutes after that before you start your workshop."

"Good," she said brightly, waiting as he slipped the bills from his wallet to pay the check. "That'll give me a chance to see how Abby feels about a roommate. Will she be in chapel?"

He glanced over at her, nodding as he pocketed his wallet, then moved to help her into the rain poncho she'd brought along.

Feeling his hands linger on her shoulders for a second longer than necessary, Freddi held her breath.

"You *are* serious?" he asked quietly before dropping his hands away.

Freddi turned to face him. "Totally. In fact, I think Abby and I will have a great time together."

Shaking his head, Mitch drew a long breath and again took her arm. "Why do I have the feeling you're absolutely right about that?" he muttered, leading her out of the dining room.

6

The man stood in the field behind the Student Center, his huge frame half-hidden behind a massive, gnarled maple tree. He kept off to the side just enough to have a good view of anyone going in or out of the Center building and the chapel across the parking lot.

Indifferent to the light rain, he watched Donovan follow the black-haired, foxy-looking woman up the walk and through the doors of the chapel, right behind the blind man and his wife.

He glanced at his watch. It was almost nine-fifteen.

There she was. As usual, the old diz came at a run, bolting out the door of the Student Center, head down against the rain. Veering to the right, she pounded across the parking lot, then went racing up the sidewalk to the chapel. He hadn't seen her walk at a normal pace yet. She always seemed to hit the pavement running.

Watching her, a knot of pressure behind his left eye began to pound in frustration. He hadn't allowed for all the fuss going on this week with this—*festival* or whatever it was. Most likely it would mean a change in the old woman's routine. From the looks of a discarded schedule he'd picked up behind the chapel earlier, there was something going on day and night.

He resented the upheaval in his plans. He'd originally intended to make his first move on her by tomorrow, or Wednesday at the latest. But now it looked like the whole campus was going to be mobbed with teachers and kids all the time. The old lady hadn't been alone for more than a few hours since yesterday.

Talk about lousy timing. He'd come expecting to find a

67

crackers old dame on her own—an open target. Instead, the place was swarming with students, and the old lady obviously had more people in her life than he'd been led to expect. In addition to the curly-headed teacher, there was a blind man and his wife sticking pretty close. And apparently the savvy looking chick with the Mercedes was part of the club as well.

His mouth twisted in a sneer as he thought of the black-haired woman. He'd just about run her off the road the day before, up by the dam. If he'd got a closer look at her, he sure wouldn't have been in such a hurry to give it up. Didn't matter, though. She seemed to be mixed up with Donovan and the old lady, so that meant he'd have to check her out. He grinned to himself. Something had to make this stupid job worthwhile.

The clincher was the rain. He was holed up in an abandoned storage shed, deep in a pine woods not too far from Donovan's and the old lady's cabins. He'd thought it would be all he needed for a few days, warm and dry and secluded. But with this rain, it was probably going to turn into a cold, wet hole real fast.

In his growing anger, a familiar crawling sensation spread over him; he could almost feel the dry, stinging rash begin to splotch his skin. Digging first at his forearms, then at his shoulders and chest, he began to carelessly rake the rash with his fingertips.

After another moment, he turned and started to walk up the incline behind the Center. Pulling his cap down a little tighter around his head, he started toward the dense, aging forest that eventually opened onto a rough path up the mountain. He zipped his black poncho all the way up to the collar, hunkering inside it against the rain as he trudged along the overgrown clearing through the woods.

He hated jobs like this. You planned and planned as tight as you could, and then it all blew up in your face because the jerk that gave the orders didn't do his homework.

Now he was going to have to blow at least another day or two just getting a fix on how many others needed handling besides the old woman. He already knew Donovan had to be terminated, but it was beginning to look as if there might be several more.

He hadn't turned up a thing at her cabin. Not that he'd really expected to. He was beginning to think this whole stinking job was a waste. His blood heated just thinking about it, and he again raked his nails over his itching forearms.

Abruptly, he remembered the cat he'd killed the night before. He had always hated cats. There'd never been less than half a dozen of them creeping around his simple-minded aunt's apartment—skinny, screeching for food, stinking up the place. He killed them off every chance he got. Remembering the one he'd wasted the night before helped to cool him down a little.

Feeling better, he took a swipe at some of the wet, low-hanging branches slapping him in the face, ignoring the pine needles that scraped his skin as he resolutely charged his way through the woods.

7

By eleven o'clock that night, Jennifer was incapable of thinking beyond a hot shower and a soft bed.

The day had turned into a true Marathon Monday: workshops in the morning and afternoon, followed by a combined contemporary Christian/gospel concert that evening. After the concert, the four of them had spent another two hours finishing the cleanup at Abby's cabin before helping Freddi move in.

Somehow they'd also managed a frenzied trip into town and a visit to Derry Ridge's only furniture store, where they had hastily purchased a new sofa bed for Abby's cabin.

Freddi's determination to buy the couch triggered what easily could have turned into a major clash between her and Mitch. Daniel, however, had thrown on the brakes with a suggestion of his own, explaining that he and Jennifer would like the opportunity to add their own efforts to those of numerous others who had already helped Abby. The end result was that Daniel paid half the purchase price of the couch, Freddi the other half.

At the moment, Jennifer would have settled for *any* couch, so long as it was close-by and out of the rain. Hurrying up the steps of the deck, she huddled gratefully against Daniel's warmth while they waited for Mitch to unlock the cabin door.

She uttered a weary moan as he pulled her under his arm and gave her a hug. "Tired?"

"I don't know which did the most damage," she admitted, "the long day or the second piece of Abby's chocolate cake."

Daniel shook his head. "You must have a real zinger of a

metabolism. By all rights, you ought to look like the Pillsbury Dough Boy, the way you eat."

Too tired to counter, Jennifer waited for Sunny to lead him through the open door, then followed.

The phone was ringing as they walked in. Mitch stopped only long enough to turn on the lamp beside the couch before starting down the hall. "I'd better answer this, in case it's Abby."

After locking the door, Jennifer went to hang up their jackets in the hall closet. When she came back, she found Daniel already sprawled out on the couch, his legs out in front of him. Beside his feet, Pork Chop was scurrying delighted circles around Sunny who merely sat, unmoving, eyeing the energetic cocker spaniel with good-natured tolerance.

Sinking down beside her husband, Jennifer watched the two dogs for a moment, then turned to Daniel. "I'm really glad you had that idea to help pay for Abby's couch. Now I feel as if we've done something to help her, too."

He nodded. "You like her a lot, don't you?"

"How could anyone *not* like Abby? She's precious."

"Well, I'm afraid there's *someone* out there who doesn't like her very much," he said grimly.

"Daniel, do you really think she's in danger?"

Locking his hands behind his head, he nodded. "It's beginning to look that way. Mitch told me tonight that Freddi's got it in her head there's a connection between the guy she saw at the musical last night and what's been happening to Abby."

"I know. She told me while we were unpacking." Jennifer shivered slightly as she recalled Freddi's detailed description of the stranger in black.

"So, what do you think of the mystery lady by now? It sounded to me as if the two of you were hitting it off pretty well tonight."

71

Straightening, Jennifer scooted closer to him. "Daniel, can you believe it? I actually helped *Gwynevere Leigh* unpack her luggage tonight. We had a *snack* together!"

"You're really impressed with her, aren't you?" he asked after a moment.

"It would be impossible not to be. Look at what she's accomplished, and she's not even thirty years old yet."

"Her books, you mean?"

"Of course, her books. She's a huge success, you know. Not to mention the fact that she's beautiful and surprisingly nice. You'd never dream she's a celebrity, would you? She's so—genuine. And did I tell you she's a Christian?"

Daniel nodded and smiled. "A couple of times."

Jennifer looked at him. "I suppose you think I'm being childish."

Still smiling, he shook his head. "A little starstruck, maybe, but not childish."

She bit her lower lip, thinking. "I don't think it's wrong to admire someone who's accomplished as much as Freddi has."

He reached for her hand. "Hey, I'm not criticizing you. I understand." Pulling her into his arms, he lightly rested his chin on top of her head. "I just hope you realize, though, that in many ways you're much more of a success than the Gwynevere Leighs of the world."

When she laughed at his foolishness, he pulled back with a frown. "I'm serious. Look at all the people in your life—the people you love and make happy. Like me. And Jason. And so many others, Jennifer. There's no index for that kind of success, but I expect the Lord rates it pretty highly. One of the things that makes you so special is your servant's heart, and I love you for it."

"What a sweet thing to say, Daniel." She lifted a hand to his bearded cheek, and he caught it and held it.

"I mean it, Jennifer. Don't minimize the importance of

what you do for other people. What about everything you've done for your family—and mine? What about those little preschoolers you teach each Sunday, and the people who get a blessing from listening to your show on the air every day, or hearing you sing in the choir at church?"

His words warmed her, but she couldn't help but wish that just once she could accomplish something *truly* special. Something important.

It would be enough, she thought, to excel in just one thing. She had her music, but even though she loved it when Daniel told her she had an "incredible" voice, she recognized the truth that her voice was better than average— but less than great. She had come to terms with that long ago.

Sometimes it just seemed that everyone in her life was doing important things, everyone except her. Daniel and his entire family were *achievers*. Athletes and teachers, musicians and physicians, craftsmen, artists, and builders— the Kaines were a mix of all kinds of gifts and abilities.

No, this was something different. Lately it seemed that everyone was doing important things, things that *mattered*— everyone except her.

The restlessness she'd felt for the past few weeks had left her frustrated. And *guilty*. The guilt, she knew, was a result of the other feelings. What in the world did she want, after all? She had a wonderful husband whom she loved more than life, an adorable son, a good Christian home—how could she *dare* to feel. . .*unfulfilled?* And yet she did.

"Jennifer?"

She jumped at the sound of Daniel's voice.

"Is something wrong?" He was still holding her hand, and now he gave it a gentle squeeze.

"Wrong?"

He nodded. "I keep getting the feeling lately that you're not entirely. . .happy."

73

Appalled that she might have hurt him or caused him concern, she quickly squeezed his hand to reassure him. "Oh, Daniel, of course I'm happy. How could I be anything but happy?"

Exactly, Jennifer. . .how could *you?*

His expression was still skeptical, and concerned. When he said nothing, she lifted her face to kiss him on the cheek. "Daniel Kaine, any woman would have to be a total fool not to be happy with a husband like you," she said firmly. "And I am *not* a foolish woman!"

He seemed to relax. Smiling a little, he held her. "It must be me, then. Maybe I'm just feeling insecure."

Jennifer studied him, but before she could question him further, Mitch appeared in the doorway.

"I'm beginning to think this week just wasn't meant to be." His expression was doleful.

Daniel apparently heard the strain in his voice. Releasing Jennifer, he got to his feet. "What's the matter, buddy?"

"That was *Lifestream's* manager on the phone. He called to cancel the group's Friday night concert. It seems their bus wrecked just outside of Nashville last night, and two of the guys are in the hospital." He paused. "Including Dylan Gray, their lead singer."

"Oh, no!" Jennifer sat forward. "How badly are they hurt?"

"Gray and the driver are listed as critical; the other guy will probably be released in a few days."

Slipping both hands into his pants pockets, Daniel asked, "What happened, do they know?"

"Head-on collision. Mason said it was an ugly night. A lot of fog and heavy rain."

Jennifer saw Daniel wince slightly, and she realized instantly that Mitch's description had jarred an ugly memory of a similar accident—the one in which Daniel had lost his sight.

74

"Apparently an elderly man went left of center and rammed into their bus," Mitch continued. He let out a long, weary sigh, then added, "That heavy rain is headed our way, incidentally."

His left shoulder lifted in a tension-relieving gesture, then dropped. Glancing at Jennifer, he said, "They were the anchor event for the entire week. Now we're going to have hundreds of people expecting a Friday night concert that isn't going to take place."

"Can't you bring in someone else?" Daniel asked.

"Not on such short notice," Mitch answered with obvious frustration.

"Why don't you do it yourself?" Daniel suggested. "You don't have to take a back seat to anyone as a musician. Get some of your kids to help put together your own concert."

Mitch stared at him incredulously. "Come on, Dan, I play a little banjo and guitar, that's all."

"*And* a little fiddle, a little mandolin, and a little dulcimer," Daniel recited dryly.

"Yeah, well, bluegrass isn't on the program. And I'm sure no CCM star. I couldn't begin to—"

He stopped in mid-sentence, his frown gradually clearing. He turned an intent, studying look on Daniel. After a moment he began to nod, slowly, then more vigorously.

"*You* could do it!"

"I could do what?" Daniel parroted blankly.

"The concert!" The worry that had darkened his eyes only an instant before suddenly lifted. "You're a natural."

His words tumbled out fast and sharp. "You're perfect for it. You've got a great voice—I heard you sing with your teen group at that youth rally in Clarksburg, remember? And you're absolute dynamite on keyboards. Plus the fact that you've got name recognition because of *Daybreak* and all your new numbers on the charts."

He stopped, a broad smile of obvious relief breaking over his features. "You'll be great!" He paused. "You *will* do it, won't you?"

Stunned by the lengthiest stream of conversation she'd yet heard from the usually taciturn Mitch, Jennifer turned to Daniel, awaiting his reaction.

"You're a maniac, man. There's no way." Daniel began to shake his head firmly. "No way."

"Now wait, Dan—listen to me a minute," Mitch said urgently. "You can bail me out on this. We're talking about mostly teens and college kids here. They'll accept you just as easily as they would *Lifestream.*"

Flicking his glance to Jennifer as if in an appeal for support, Mitch continued to press. "You've got a lot more credibility with your music than you seem to realize, Dan. Once people find out who you are—that you're the man behind *Daybreak*—well, that's all it'll take. Trust me."

Daniel leaned toward Mitch in an attempt to protest, but the suddenly persuasive Mitch wasn't finished.

"You're exactly what I need. Where else could I get someone who could just walk on and take over on such short notice?"

"Mitchell, do you think you could just listen to me for a minute here? Please?" Daniel assumed the tone of voice he ordinarily used with Jason when he was trying to explain a very difficult point. "It's true that I've done some stuff with my teen ensembles at youth rallies. *But—*" he slowed his words, giving each one a deliberate emphasis— "they are not here this week. All you have are me and a few instruments. And that, my friend, does not a concert make."

"You've got Jennifer," Mitch countered without missing a beat. Turning to her, he said, "Dan's told me about your voice. You studied in Rome, didn't you? I can't wait to hear the two of you together."

Jennifer opened her mouth to protest, but Mitch waved off

76

her attempt. "The Lord *does* provide. You guys are going to save it for me."

"Hey, Mitch—" Daniel tried again.

"I wouldn't even *think* of getting up there in front of all those people!" Jennifer broke in. "For goodness sake, Mitch, I sing in our church choir—that's all!"

Daniel turned toward her. "Don't go putting yourself down, Jennifer. You've got an absolutely incredible voice."

"Daniel—"

Mitch narrowed his eyes at her. "If Dan will do it, will you?"

"No, I will *not*! Daniel, tell him I won't—"

"I wouldn't even consider doing it alone," Daniel said stubbornly.

"There you are, Jennifer." Mitch's tone was both earnest and solemn. "The ball's in your court."

Jennifer stared at him. Undaunted, Mitch simply shot her a boyish, thoroughly disarming grin.

"Besides," he rushed to add before Jennifer could say anything, "neither of you can say no without at least *praying* about it, can you? I mean, how do you know this isn't the real reason you're here this week? Maybe this is exactly why the Lord led you to Derry Ridge."

Jennifer looked at him incredulously, then turned to Daniel. Her stomach did a slow flip when she saw the frown of uncertainty on her husband's face. Mitch's outburst had obviously hit a nerve.

"All right, all right. We'll pray about it," Daniel conceded.

"*Daniel!*"

Both shoulders went up in a shrug of helplessness. "He's right, Jennifer. What if this *is* the reason we're here this week?"

Jennifer gaped at him for another moment, then turned back to Mitch. Intending to level one of her most piercing glares on him, she hesitated, stopped by a sudden flash of

77

insight about the lean-faced, gentle-natured Kentuckian.

While Mitch Donovan might very well possess what Daniel had rather whimsically described as the "spirit of a poet and the heart of a Christian martyr," the gleeful, outrageous grin he now turned on Jennifer was that of an Irish sea captain about to board the enemy's ship.

Jennifer knew with a sudden, unnerving certainty that she and Daniel would be doing the Friday night concert.

8

Freddi awoke before dawn the following morning to the sound of rain pounding relentlessly on the roof of Abby's cabin.

Instantly alert, she swung her legs over the side of the sofa bed and reached for the jeans and cotton pullover she'd laid out the night before. The room was cool, and she dressed hurriedly, then went to the front window to look out.

There was little to see. Mitch had replaced the security light the night before, but it was wrapped too thickly by the mountain's dense fog and a heavy curtain of rain to be little more than a feeble beacon in the darkness.

Eventually she turned away, crossing the room to turn on a lamp beside the sofa. The small living room was snug and friendly in the warm glow from the lamp. Mitch's touch was everywhere. Last night, after the others had gone, Abby had pointed out to Freddi a number of pieces which he had either built or refinished: the blue milk-chair resting against the opposite wall; the double-board mantel above a rebricked fireplace; the wide-planked floor he'd stained to a satin finish, then accented with a multi-colored hooked rug from a local estate auction. Even most of the primitive tin and local stoneware pieces on the mantel had come from his own collection.

Smiling a little to herself as she let her gaze scan the room, Freddi reached for a treasure of her own. Picking up a small figurine music box from the lamp table where she'd placed it the night before, she traced with loving gentleness the graceful lines of a barefoot young girl in a ballgown. Mounted on a pedestal meant to resemble a patch of wild flowers, the girl had long black hair and enormous eyes and was playing a wooden flute.

Mitch had given it to her on her sixteenth birthday. He had stood there, home from college just for her birthday, handsome but still too thin, watching her intently to measure her reaction.

"... *It was so much like you I couldn't resist it,*" she could still hear him saying. "*Classic country.*" His smile had been tender but uncertain. What she hadn't realized at the time was that the music box was imported porcelain and had most likely set him back an entire month's salary.

With great care and a faintly sad smile, Freddi turned the figurine, winding it just enough to start the music. Eyes shut, she listened to the soft, plaintive tune of *Derry Air,* the song known around the world as *Danny Boy.*

Freddi had slept in dozens of hotel rooms, lived in New York, Chicago, and, for a few months, San Francisco. She'd seen most of the United States, traveled to England, Ireland, Scotland, and Wales. And everywhere she went, the music box had gone with her. From place to place, year to year, night after night, she had kept it with her and, with it, the memory of Mitch. . . .

When she opened her eyes, they were filled with tears which she resolutely blinked away as she replaced the figurine on the table. She would tuck it away in her things later, before Mitch could happen in and see it, but not just yet.

Leaving the room, she padded down the hall to the kitchen in her stocking feet.

A dim light was glowing weakly just inside the kitchen door, enough for Freddi to find her way around. Crossing to the counter, she plugged in the coffee maker Abby had filled the night before, then opened the cabinet above the sink to get a cup.

There was a brass hanging lamp over the small oval table. She started across the room to turn it on, stopping first at the window. Pulling the curtain back a little, she looked out, then down, in the direction of Mitch's cabin.

Last night she'd been able to see his roof and one side of the deck from this same window, but not this morning; the rain-veiled darkness made for near zero visibility. She thought she *did* see a faint glow of light coming from the cabin and stood watching it for a moment, wondering if Mitch was awake.

The coffee maker gurgled and choked, and she glanced over her shoulder toward the counter, then turned back to the window. A slight movement in the distance caught her attention, and she stepped closer, bringing her nose almost against the glass as she strained to see.

Off to the right, about halfway down between the two cabins, something moved. As she watched, she realized she'd been wrong about the light she'd seen a moment ago. It wasn't coming from inside Mitch's cabin, but rather the outside.

And it was moving. Suspended eerily in the darkness for several seconds, it flickered, then began to flutter away from the cabin.

With growing uneasiness, Freddi finally began to realize what she was seeing. Somebody was down there with a lantern or a flashlight, somebody who was now starting up the mountain.

Her mind raced. What kind of crazy would be coming up the mountain before daylight—and in this kind of weather?

Instinctively, she backed away, then bolted across the kitchen to turn off the night light. With the room now in total darkness, she crept back to the window. More cautiously this time, she again nudged the curtain to one side.

The light was still there. Like an oversized, menacing firefly emerging out of the rain-draped woods, it was swaying and weaving its way up the mountain, toward Abby's cabin.

Freddi's throat tightened. Her eyes scanned the sky,

81

hoping for at least a pale tracing of light, but it was still midnight dark.

As she watched, the light suddenly changed directions. Veering off to the right, it began to drift toward the other side of the Ridge. After a few more seconds, it disappeared from her field of vision.

Chilled, Freddi stepped back from the window, thinking about what she'd seen. Somebody had been outside—

She swallowed. Somebody could have been *inside.*

Moving quickly but silently, she crossed the room, fumbling through the drawers on either side of the sink until she finally located a small flashlight. Aiming the light low until she reached the wall phone beside the refrigerator, she lifted the handset and trained the flashlight on the insert card. As she'd hoped, Mitch's number was there, the first one listed.

She keyed in the number with an unsteady hand, pulling in a couple of deep breaths as she waited.

Let him be all right, Lord. . .please, let him be all right.

Mitch answered on the second ring.

"Mitch—are you all right?"

"Freddi?" He sounded disoriented, only half-awake. "What's wrong?"

"Mitch, listen to me—are you awake—I saw something— somebody—outside your cabin," she said, her voice low but urgent.

"What?" His tone was gruff but alert. "When?"

"A few minutes ago. I was in the kitchen, looking out the window, and I saw a light. At first I thought it was coming from inside your cabin, but then it started moving, coming up the mountain. Whoever it was came about halfway up and then headed west."

There was silence for an instant, then, "Are you sure?"

"*Yes,* I'm sure. That's why I called you."

82

"That's all you could see—a light?"

"It's too dark to see anything else."

"All right," he said after a moment. "I'll have a look." He stopped, then asked, "You and Abby are both all right?"

"We're fine. Abby's still asleep." She paused, then cautioned, "Mitch, be careful."

He grunted something unintelligible and hung up.

As soon as Mitch hung up the phone, he shrugged into his clothes and hurried downstairs, almost colliding with Dan in the living room.

"Sunny barked a couple of times a few minutes earlier," Dan explained, "so I took her out of the bedroom before she could wake Jennifer. She's settled down now," he added. "I don't know what she heard."

It occured to Mitch that Pork Chop must also have been restless in the night. The cocker had been on the couch when Mitch went to bed, but he'd moved to the bedroom sometime before Freddi's phone call.

Mitch waited until Dan and Sunny returned to the bedroom before going outside. Dan would have insisted on going with him, and there was no point in him getting drenched, too. Besides, he felt no particular uneasiness about whatever Freddi had seen. She had always looked for the weird stuff first, before seeking a natural explanation. Chances were she'd seen the flashlight of a stranded motorist or maybe even the reflection of someone's headlights. He expected to find nothing outside.

Twenty minutes later he was behind the wheel of the Ranger, heading up the mountain toward Abby's place. He'd seen nothing during his ten minute search that looked suspicious. There *had* been a sunken dip of mud not far from the back porch that looked as if someone might have slipped or skidded, but with the ground so spongy, there was no telling what might have caused it. No point in jumping to

83

conclusions just because Freddi was feeling skittish.

Besides, who would be fool enough to go traipsing around in this miserable weather before daylight?

Someone who didn't want to be seen. . . .

He tried to push the nagging thought away. He was cold, still sleepy, and mildly irritated with Freddi for getting him out of bed in the first place. All things considered, it was no wonder the dull headache he'd gotten up with was growing worse by the minute.

His headlights were nearly useless in the fog, and the windshield wipers slapping furiously at the wind-driven downpour weren't keeping up with the rain blowing across the glass. By the time he pulled into the turnaround at Abby's cabin, he was gritting his teeth with tension.

Raising the hood of his warmup jacket, he leaped from the truck and made a run for the porch. Freddi opened the door before he could knock. "Give me your jacket," she whispered as he stepped inside.

He shook his head. "I'll put it in the bathroom so it can dry out. Is Abby still asleep?"

She nodded, saying, "There's coffee in the kitchen."

As soon as he walked into the kitchen, she handed him a steaming mug of black coffee, then turned to refill her own cup.

Leaning against the counter, he watched her, his mouth going dry in spite of the coffee. Her hair was piled carelessly on top of her head, loosely secured with some sort of foreign object that resembled a twisted knitting needle. Her nose was shiny, her eyes still smudged with sleep. She looked scrubbed, innocent, and extremely young.

She was wearing some kind of soft-looking cotton shirt—pink—and an old pair of jeans. No shoes. He found himself wondering if she still hated shoes. Did she go barefoot in her apartment in Chicago? Freddi had always had a dislike for anything that restricted her movement. Uncomfortable shoes, tight clothing, even gloves had been odious to her.

Embarrassed, he realized he'd been staring when he saw her staring curiously at *him*. Apparently she had asked him a question.

"Mitch?"

"Sorry. It takes me a while to wake up."

"I asked if you found anything."

He shook his head. "Nothing." He took another sip of coffee, then went to sit down at the table.

She followed, scooting into a chair directly across from him.

"So—do you think someone was watching your cabin?"

He looked at her and, seeing the familiar intensity in those wide gray eyes, could almost hear the gears grinding in that imagination of hers. "In this rain? More likely it was someone stranded on the road, someone looking for a telephone."

"Did you pass anyone on your way here?"

"No, but they could have been farther up."

Her eyes met his over the rim of her cup as she took a sip of coffee. "You don't really believe that."

"I *do* believe it, and you'd better do likewise. Give it up Freddi," he said, suddenly impatient with her. "You're not going to find any new plot ideas on the Ridge."

She seemed unruffled by his dig. "Oh, I don't know. I'd say this one is beginning to show a lot of promise."

"Such as?" he challenged.

She smiled at him. "Such as. . .One: a weird-looking stranger shows up on the Ridge—for no apparent reason. Two: Someone shoots out Abby's security light—for no apparent reason. Three: Unknown subject rips up Abby's cabin and kills her pet cat—for no apparent reason. Four: Someone waving a flashlight sneaks away from your cabin in the middle of a pre-dawn downpour—for no apparent reason. . . ."

85

He threw up a hand to stop her. "All right, all right. We've got some stuff that's out of the ordinary."

Neither of them said anything more for a few moments. Finally, Freddi got up and took both their cups to the counter for a refill. He watched her, grudgingly admitting to himself that coincidence couldn't possibly cover all the unexplained events of the past two days.

"So what's your point, Freddi-Leigh?" The familiar combination of her two names into one slipped out before he could stop it. The nickname he'd given her years ago had been a teasing endearment he no longer had the right to use.

Apparently, she hadn't noticed. With smooth, unhurried movements, she poured fresh coffee and returned to the table, looking totally at ease and unaffected.

She sat down, then took a long, cautious sip of hot coffee. "My point," she said evenly, "is that Abby may be in a great deal of danger." Her eyes met his and held. "And if I were writing this story, your involvement with Abby would place you in jeopardy right along with her."

Startled, he almost laughed, then saw that she was completely serious. Combing the damp hair at the back of his neck with his fingers, he wondered tiredly how his life, so orderly and routine only a few days ago, had suddenly become so turbulent and complicated.

It was easy to blame Freddi for the turbulence, not quite so easy to blame her for all the complications.

At the touch of her fingers on his wrist, his head shot up.

"Mitch? You look exhausted. Why don't you go back to your place and try to get some more sleep?"

He shook his head, unable to drag his eyes away from the long slender fingers touching his wrist. "It's too late. I'd just feel worse the second time up."

She withdrew her hand, and, for an instant, he wanted to

recapture it. Abruptly, he stood, pushing his chair back to the table before downing the last sip of coffee remaining in his cup. "I'd better go."

Freddi rose from her chair, reaching for his empty cup and taking it with hers to the sink. "Is there a photography lab on campus?" she asked, turning back to him.

He nodded. "In Fletcher Hall—the language arts building. Why?"

She came back to the table. "What about a fax machine?"

Again he gave a small nod. "There's a new one in the administration office."

"If I can reach Henderson this morning—that's the PI I told you about—he's going to want photographs," she explained. "I've got a picture of our man in black; I took it the other evening at the musical. If Abby will let me, I'll take a couple of shots of her this morning. I'd like to get them developed as soon as possible and fax them to Chicago."

"That shouldn't be any problem. If you give me the film this morning, I can get someone to develop it before noon."

"Great. Mitch—"

He was finding it inexplicably difficult to look at her, as if he were afraid of being caught in the force field of her eyes.

"I'm only trying to help. You *do* understand that, don't you? I *like* Abby."

Carefully avoiding her gaze, he managed a weak smile. "That's good. She's really happy about your being here."

"I wish you were."

For a moment he thought he'd only imagined her soft return, that she really hadn't said it. He took a step away from her, then stopped, willing himself to meet her eyes.

He wasn't sure what he was looking for as he searched her face, had no idea what he thought to find. He only knew there was something new in her eyes, something that hadn't been

87

there when they were younger. A quiet kind of strength, a steady composure seemingly reinforced by a new sense of peace pervading her every word, her every gesture.

It almost made him angry—this unfamiliar . . . *quietness* about her. She had walked back into his life without warning, plunging him heart-deep in a backwash of painful memories and broken dreams. And when she grew tired of whatever game she was playing at the moment, she would once again walk *out* of his life, leaving him to drown in the current she'd set in motion. It would be just like before: Freddi would go on, and he would stay. Alone.

In an effort to temper the anxiety rapidly boiling up in him, he began to talk as they headed for the living room, telling her about *Lifestream's* accident, his concern about the approaching Friday night concert, and his plea to Daniel for assistance.

"Do you think he'll do it?"

"He promised to tell me this morning," he answered, fishing his keys out of his pocket as they walked into the dimly lighted living room. "I don't know what I'll do if he decides not to—"

He stopped, staring with disbelief at the table next to the sofa.

A fist began to hammer at his chest, then moved to his throat, choking him. Unable to move, unable to speak, he stood there, his eyes locked on the music box. It was as if all the shattered pieces of their past, all the dusty, elusive dreams they'd shared together, were slowly rising from the ashes.

Stiffly, he took a step toward the table, then another. Finally, he reached for the music box, touched it, picked it up and studied it.

"I. . .was showing it to Abby last night," Freddi said in an unsteady voice. "I meant to put it away. . .later."

He tried to swallow, but the fist was still lodged in his throat.

He wanted to hold her. He wanted to shout at her.

"It still plays," she said, her words little more than a whisper.

Finally she moved toward him, reaching for the music box. He glanced down at it once, then handed it to her.

Taking it, she wound it very slowly, lifting her face to his and smiling a little as the music began to chime.

Emotion swelled in him, threatening to explode. He moved to touch her, even while his mind shouted its warning, *Don't. . .this is just a diversion for her. . .don't set yourself up for the pain again.*

She was only inches away from him, and he reached for her. His hand went to her hair, then hesitated when she closed her eyes. He touched one long, silken strand, wrapping it around his fingers, then watching it slowly fall free.

Her eyes opened, traveling over his face, and he almost reeled at the memories he saw reflected there. For a moment the rain beating down on the tiny cabin became his heartbeat, drumming the past back into existence, crashing through every survival wall he'd spent months and years building.

Inanely, he blurted out, "I have to go now."

She hesitated only an instant, studying him with a level, measuring gaze. "I'll get your jacket," she said quietly, turning to leave the room.

When he walked out onto the porch, she followed him. It was still raining, but a weak gray light was now creeping over the sky.

"Have there been any reports on the river yet?" she asked, hugging her arms tightly to her body.

"No. They'll probably start them this afternoon." He glanced into the downpour, avoiding her gaze. "You might want to keep an eye on Abby once they start issuing the flood warnings. She has a thing about the river. You may have to reassure her."

At her questioning look, he said, "I don't know what it is. She just doesn't like the river. She won't go near it."

"Some sort of phobia, do you think?"

He shrugged. "I guess. She likes to keep her distance from it, that's for sure."

Still averting his eyes, he stepped off the porch. "Is it all right if Abby rides in with you this morning?"

"Of course."

"She usually goes in around seven, but not today. Let her sleep for awhile and come in with you at nine. I'll tell the other ladies in the cafeteria."

Back inside the Ranger, he punched the key into the ignition and started the engine, waiting for it to warm up before pulling out.

As he watched, Freddi waved, then stepped back inside and closed the door.

Mitch put the truck in gear and started down the mud-slickened mountain road, the refrain of *Danny Boy* playing in his mind and tugging at his heart.

9

Huddled inside his poncho, the man perched Indian style on a blanket in the back of the van. The blanket was already wet from his drenched clothing, and the poncho was next to worthless for warmth. Late last night he'd abandoned the ramshackle storage shed and gone after the van, deciding it would provide better shelter from the rain than the drafty, mud-floored shed.

He figured there were vans all over the place in a hick college town like this; no one was going to pay any attention to one more. Besides, once he was done with the old diz and her friends, the sooner he could get out of this mud hole, the better.

In spite of the miserable wet chill of the morning, his skin felt hot, almost feverish from the rage and frustration simmering inside him. The skin rash was worse than it had been for years; his left eye was infected again—probably because of the weeds he'd been tramping around in; and his gut was on fire from all the acid he was churning.

Scowling, he glanced around the van's dark interior. Here he sat, a rich man by anybody's standards with three foreign bank accounts and a couple of others in Dade County. He should be staying in a first class hotel—he could take his pick—instead of hunkering out here in the woods like some wild animal.

Rolling his shoulders and neck sideways to relieve the stiffness, he reminded himself why he was putting up with this garbage. It was big bucks—he already had the first fat installment, and he stood to collect twice that once he finished things here. The jerk who was financing the whole thing had accused him of messing up the first time, but he'd

91

straightened him out real quick.

Dabbing at his eye with a clean handkerchief, he snorted to himself. Poor old Taylor hadn't flapped his mouth for long. It had taken only a couple of minutes to make the little wimp understand the facts. He hadn't messed up—Catchside never messed up a job, not this one or any other. This week was nothing more than a loose end, that's all. He was doing it because *he* wanted to, not because some pencil-pushing lightweight was leaning on him.

He'd finish the job for the rest of the bucks and for his own satisfaction. Thinking about the ones he'd have to waste besides the old lady—he decided the rest of the week just might not be all grief. Maybe he'd get some laughs out of this after all.

He usually did.

Abby was having the dream again.

Her bedroom. . .the entire cabin. . .was filled with dark water. Cold water, black, opaque, and inhabited by. . .*things*. . . things that didn't belong. . .people she didn't know. . .eyes following her, glaring at her, accusing her. . .guns. . .and blood. . .blood filled water. . . .

Then came the shadow, an enormous black shadow rising up from the water. . .no, not a shadow, a man. . .a mammoth hulk of a man with white hair and black clothes, black like the water. . . .

He was struggling, grappling with another man, a man in a white shirt. . .she knew this man, he was good, made her feel safe. . .there was a girl between them, a pretty young girl with a blonde pony tail and pink tennis shoes. . . .

Abby tried to scream at them, warn them about the man with the gun. . .they were going to get hurt. . .she opened her mouth and screamed and screamed, but nothing came out. . . .She tried to run, to warn them, to help them, but her legs were so heavy and all she could do was float. . .float in the water. . . .

She heard the explosion and again tried to scream, but the black water choked off her voice, filled her throat, and her lungs. . . .

Blood. . .the water was turning to blood. . .a white shirt drifted by, white stained with red. . .then a pink tennis shoe. . .and another. . . .

Now beyond her she saw the man, the one with the gun. . .he was in the water, raging like a furious sea monster, blood on his shirt, on his face, in his hair. . .he grabbed her legs, pushed his face close to hers. . . .

His eyes. . .he had no eyes. . . .

She screamed, and this time the sound finally ripped free from her throat as she shot up and forward in bed.

Arms went around her, holding her close as a voice—a gentle voice—said kind, soothing things to her, warming her from the cold, icy terror in which the dark water had wrapped her.

It was Freddi, Mitch's Freddi. Freddi was here. The water was gone. Abby told her about the dream, and Freddi held her until she was warm again.

10

"I've been wanting to ask you this ever since we met," Jennifer said, finally giving in to her curiosity. "How in the world did you get a nickname like 'Freddi'?"

Driving with one hand on the steering wheel, her left arm on the ledge of the door, Freddi glanced over at her. "Mitch gave it to me," she said, laughing softly. "He always said I was too much of a tomboy for a name like 'Gwynevere'."

The two of them were on their way back to the cabins, having spent an hour at the small shopping center just outside of town buying toiletries for themselves and a few groceries for Abby.

Turning off the main highway onto the narrow, snakelike road that scaled the mountain, Freddi shifted to low gear, saying, "You and I have the same name, you know."

Jennifer shot her a questioning look.

" 'Gwynevere'—in a variety of spellings—is an old Welsh name," Freddi explained, turning her gaze back to the road. "It evolved into several different forms over the centuries. One is 'Jennifer'. Another is 'Winifred'. Mitch found out about that one and dubbed me 'Freddi'. It stuck all the way through school."

"The two of you went to school together?"

"Mm-hm. Well, in a way. Mitch is four years older than I am, but he was always—around. I really *was* a tomboy," she said, again looking at Jennifer with a quick smile, "forever getting myself into situations I couldn't get out of. Mitch just always seemed to be there to bail me out. Over the years he settled into a role somewhere between big brother and guardian."

"That would be nice," Jennifer said. "I have two brothers,

94

but they're both younger. I often wondered what it would be like to have an older brother who'd take care of *me* for a change."

"I used to daydream about having a whole houseful of brothers and sisters," Freddi said. "My parents were killed in an airplane crash when I was in elementary school, and a couple of years later my grandmother died. That left just Grandpa and me. I loved having Mitch hover over me— except when he got too bossy, of course—but my grandfather wasn't keen on the arrangement. He never approved of Mitch."

Surprised, Jennifer wondered how anyone could disapprove of Mitch.

Freddi grimaced when the Mercedes bounced over a huge pothole, shooting muddy water several feet high over the car. "Grandpa was a good man," she said, turning the windshield wipers on high, "but he had an almost obsessive sense of family pride. He could trace his ancestors all the way back to the original Kentucky settlers, and he had a real problem with people like the 'Do-nothing Donovans,' as he called them."

She glanced over at Jennifer. "He got worse when Mitch and I started dating. He didn't actually forbid us to see one another—he just made life miserable for Mitch every time he came around."

"But he continued to come?" Jennifer prompted. She could hardly wait to tell Daniel that she'd been right about the romance between these two.

"Oh, yes," Freddi said with a reminiscent grin. "In his own way, Mitch was a match for Grandpa. At least in terms of stubbornness."

Pulling onto the gravel drive in front of Mitch's cabin, she put the car in park, letting the engine idle. "Grandpa was never able to see the goodness in Mitch," she said softly, staring out the window. "He was so hung up on what most people *think* is important that he never looked quite far enough to see what *is* important."

Thinking about her words, Jennifer nodded. "I guess we all do that sometimes."

"Sure we do. That's why I left the Ridge."

Jennifer looked at her.

"I grew up restless," Freddi said, sinking back against the car seat as she continued to gaze out the front windshield. "I can't remember a time when I didn't want to escape the Ridge, to go—exploring. I just *knew*," she said, turning to Jennifer with a humorless smile, "that there were all kinds of wonderful, exciting things waiting for me on the other side of this mountain. And I was determined to find every one of them—career, success, excitement—I wanted it all. Everything Derry Ridge didn't have."

"And you found it," Jennifer said, wondering at the disconsolate look that had settled over Freddi's pretty features.

Freddi met her eyes for a long moment, then looked away. "I found it. But a few months ago I began to realize that I'd lost far more than I'd found."

"And that's why you came back?" Jennifer studied Freddi's profile, puzzled by the regret and disillusionment she sensed there.

"Nothing seemed important to me any longer," Freddi answered. "I'd always been restless, unsettled—but this was different. Nothing satisfied me, nothing mattered to me—not even my writing. I felt as if . . . as if I had no *reality* in my life. Everything had become so artificial—so *plastic*."

There was no self-pity or resentment in her words, merely a quiet steadiness as she went on. "For the first time in—too long—I began to really pray." She looked at Jennifer. "Until then I'd only been giving lip service to my relationship with the Lord. My writing had always come first—always. Everything else—including God—took second place."

As Jennifer listened, she began to sense that this was the first time Freddi had actually talked her way through her feelings. It was almost as if she were speaking to herself, so simple and sincere were her words.

"I realize now that I was passing through a kind of crisis in my faith, a turning point. I was forced to face the truth about myself: the center of my existence had never been Christ, even though I'd been a Christian since I was seven."

Her gaze grew distant and more contemplative. "It was a devastating time for me. I was brought to a place of stark, raw honesty about what I believed and why I believed it. Gradually I began to realize that Christ had been my Savior for years— but I hadn't wanted Him as my *Lord.* He had never," she added in a voice that was little more than a whisper, "really been *first* in my life."

She was silent for another moment. Finally she spoke, and her words arrowed straight to Jennifer's heart.

"You see, I had to get to the place where Jesus was enough. I had to reach the point where I could say, and mean it with all my being, that if I lost everything—my writing, my success, my health, *everything*—I would still have something. . .Someone. . .at the very center of my life who would be enough."

Shaken, Jennifer suddenly glimpsed a different Freddi. Or was she simply seeing the *whole* Freddi. A somewhat lonely, wounded young woman, a woman with eyes that held yesterday's sorrows and no small measure of pain. But beyond that she sensed the very essence of peace, a peace that came only from what Daniel called the *sufficiency of Christ.*

Somewhere at the back of her mind, an uneasy question began to form, a question about her own peace. Could it be that she had allowed her feelings of inadequacy, her recent frustration and dissatisfaction, to invade that peace? Had she, like Freddi, forgotten that Jesus was enough?

Guiltily, she allowed her mind to replay Freddi's words: *"Someone. . .at the very center of my life who would be enough. . . ."*

That didn't apply to her, she silently insisted. She had given the Lord first place in her life long ago.

Then how was she to account for the recent feelings of discontent that nagged at her?

Freddi's voice broke into her thoughts. "Oh no! I can't believe it's after five already. We're going to have to hustle to make the concert tonight."

Jennifer glanced at her watch and groaned. "I promised to start dinner for Mitch! And I wanted to call and check on Jason, too." Collecting her purse, she turned to Freddi. "You and Abby are still coming for dinner, aren't you?"

"I'll drop Abby off, but I'm not staying. In fact, I think I'm going to skip tonight's concert, too; I've got some things I want to do at the farm. By the way," she said dryly, "what's this I hear about you and Daniel doing a concert of your own Friday night?"

Jennifer made a face. "I didn't realize Mitch could be such a hard-sell. I can't believe he actually talked Daniel into it."

"You'll be super," Freddi assured her, smiling. "I'm glad you're doing it."

"*Daniel* is doing it," Jennifer corrected, opening the door. "I'll be in the front row, rooting for him."

Freddi grinned at her. "Somehow I think your husband may have other ideas."

Jennifer started to get out, then turned back. "Are you going to need any help tonight? I could go with you."

Freddi shook her head. "It won't take long. I just want to move a few things upstairs in case we get water."

"Water?"

Freddi nodded. "This is a flood district. It's easy to forget about it up here"—she inclined her head toward the upper part of the mountain—"but the farm's too close to the

98

bottoms for comfort. The house has never taken much damage, but the first floor *has* had water a couple of times."

"You're not going to try to move furniture?"

"No, just some small stuff I'd hate to see ruined. I can prop most of the furniture up off the floor."

"Mitch will be disappointed if you don't stay," Jennifer said without thinking.

Freddi straightened in the seat, waiting for Jennifer to get out. "Most likely," she replied with a rueful smile, "Mitch will be relieved."

Five minutes later, Jennifer was appraising the contents of Mitch's refrigerator. When the telephone rang, she answered it with one hand, reaching with her free hand to set a plastic container of lettuce on the butcher block counter.

It was Freddi. "Jennifer, is Abby there?"

"Abby? No. At least I don't think so. I've been in the kitchen ever since I came inside, but I'm fairly certain she's not here."

"She's not here either."

Hearing the concern in Freddi's voice, Jennifer glanced through the open doorway into the hall. "Hold on a minute, and I'll check the rest of the cabin," she said, laying the handset on the counter.

After finding no sign of Abby anywhere in the cabin, Jennifer picked up the extension in Mitch's bedroom. "She's not here, Freddi. Maybe she went back to the campus for something."

There was a pause, then, "Mitch told her not to go anywhere alone."

"Do you think we should call him?"

Again Freddi hesitated. "Would you mind looking around outside? I'll do the same up here. If neither of us finds her, then I'll call the campus." She paused. "Did Mitch give you any idea what time he planned to come back to the cabin?"

"About six. He and Daniel were going to meet with a few students in the choir and try to put together a backup ensemble for Friday night. Listen, I'll go outside right now. I'll call you back—"

"No, if I don't find her in the next few minutes I'll come down. Otherwise I'll call you."

After grabbing her rain jacket, Jennifer exchanged her dress shoes for a pair of ankle boots, and headed for the back door.

Stepping out onto the deck, she glanced around, then hurried down the steps into the yard, starting for the garage at the rear of the cabin.

It was raining again. She pulled up the hood of her jacket before dashing across the walk to the garage. Peering through the window that ran the length of the garage door, she could see nothing but a few small tools hanging on a pegboard and a couple of spare tires leaning against the far wall.

Turning, she scanned her surroundings. Mitch's back yard was actually part of the mountain. He had cleared less than an acre for his own use directly from the slope, and his lot line merged naturally with the tree-covered hillside. There was a small, white barn directly across from the garage, separated by only a few feet of gravel.

Tugging the zipper of her jacket all the way to her throat, Jennifer raced across the gravel to the front of the barn. The door was locked, so she went around to the side, her feet sinking a good inch in the mud.

"You could have used a little gravel over here, too, Mitch," she mumbled to herself.

Cupping her hands, she framed her eyes and tried to see through the narrow, mud-splashed window at the side of the barn. It was dark inside, and the window was filthy. She

100

squinted, waiting for her eyes to focus. Gradually, she made out the dim shapes of a lawnmower and a bicycle resting against the wall. A workshop bench with numerous power tools spanned the far end of the barn.

Remaining under the building's overhang, out of the rain, Jennifer turned and looked around once more. Obviously, Abby was nowhere near; she decided to go back inside in case Freddi should call.

She started toward the cabin, then stopped. Out of the corner of her eye she saw something move, off to her right. She turned to look. A man in a black, billowing rain poncho was trudging resolutely up the mountain. He was several yards away, his back to her.

Her breath caught in her throat. It had to be Freddi's Monster Man. There was no mistaking someone his size. He was walking fast, his tree-trunk legs covering the rise in giant steps. An undeniable aura of menace issued from him as his massive, black-clad figure sludged upward.

Jennifer hesitated only a moment before moving. Racing across the graveled section of the yard, she dipped in among the trees, taking care to stay concealed as she began to edge her way up the mud-slicked hillside.

The man was over a hundred yards up the mountain from her by now, but Jennifer still had a clear view of his back as he continued to climb. The wind had picked up and was slashing through the trees, hurling the rain with a force that made her face sting with pain. Her heart was pumping hard, more from apprehension than exertion. She knew she ought to go back, but she *had* to see where he was going.

About halfway up to Abby's cabin, where the woods broke into a narrow clearing for a few feet, he suddenly turned left and began to jog, head down against the wind-driven rain.

Jennifer tried to increase her own pace, clutching at tree branches as she climbed to keep from losing her balance on the slippery incline, ducking her head every few seconds to protect her face from the slapping tree limbs. She gulped air greedily, now veering left as she strained to keep the man in sight.

The distance between them was rapidly widening. In order to keep him in view, she was going to have to sacrifice the refuge of the woods and break into the clearing. It would mean leaving herself open, risking his seeing her, but she was going to lose sight of him otherwise.

Her chest was on fire, the palms of her hands raw and wet. Making her decision, she broke forward, leaving the covering of the woods for open ground.

The man was almost out of sight. Jennifer began to run. The mud sucked at her feet, pulling at her, slowing her pace.

Unexpectedly, the man slowed, then turned and started toward the edge of another wooded area, heading toward a dilapidated, unpainted storage barn nearly concealed by trees. A black van was pulled in close to it, its front half nosed in snugly among the trees.

Jennifer stopped, watching. The man went directly to the back of the van, unlocked it, and opened the doors. He raised one leg to climb inside, then stopped, looking around as if he'd heard something.

Jennifer caught her breath on a choked cry of panic as he turned and stood scanning his surroundings. Below a black shooter's cap his face was pasty, his eyes concealed by dark glasses.

She tried to dart away from the clearing and back into the trees before he could see her, but as she bolted toward the woods her foot caught in the mud. Her ankle twisted hard and she went down, pitching forward between two enormous pine trees. She fell on her side and shoved a fist hard against her mouth to keep from screaming.

She realized with relief that she wasn't hurt, only stunned

and badly jarred. Praying the man hadn't seen her, she scrambled to her feet, grabbing a low-hanging branch to steady herself. After an instant she released the branch, and, half-sliding, half-running, fled down the side of the hill. Weaving her way through the trees, she glanced over her shoulder every few seconds as she ran.

Suddenly, she heard tree branches slapping somewhere nearby.

He had seen her. . .he was coming after her.

Mindless of the pain, she grabbed branches with hands already bloody, choking on the taste of her own terror as she heard the thrashing sounds closing in on her. Her heart was exploding, threatening to bang its way through her rib cage.

She whipped around to look behind her and skidded into a tree hard enough to knock the breath from her.

Stunned, she squeezed her eyes shut against the hot pain stabbing at her shoulder as she leaned weakly back against the tree. Exhausted and disoriented, she squeezed her eyes shut to blot the tears that, mingled with the rain, were nearly blinding her.

He was close, so close she could hear the sound of his footsteps moving nearer, slower now.

Dear Lord, help me get away. . . .

"Jennifer!"

She opened her eyes to see Freddi dart out from between two trees and come running toward her. The hood of her raincoat had fallen away, and her hair was a wet black cape hugging her head.

Freddi grabbed Jennifer's shoulders. "What happened? Are you all right?" Her eyes raked Jennifer's face with a mixture of fear and concern.

Unable to speak, Jennifer could only stare blankly. Shivering hard, she tried to form words but managed only a choked sob.

Freddi's hands tightened on her shoulders. "Jennifer, are you hurt?" she asked, her voice urgent.

Shaking her head stiffly, Jennifer was finally able to answer. "I thought you were him. . . ."

"Who? You thought I was who?"

"You know. . .the man you saw the other night. . .the one you called 'Monster Man'. . . ."

She heard the violent tremor in her voice but couldn't stop shaking. Balling her fists, she tried to control the spasms racking her body. "He was behind. . .the cabin. . . . I tried to follow him. . .to see where he went. . .I thought he was coming after me."

Steadying her with a firm arm, Freddi scanned the woods, her eyes darting everywhere at once. "He was here? You saw him?"

Jennifer stared at her. "We have to get out of here! He may have seen me!" She strained, pulling free of Freddi. "*Hurry!*"

Freddi grabbed Jennifer's arm, holding onto it as they ran. "Are you sure you're all right?" she asked again, glancing over her shoulder as they stumbled down the hill.

"Yes. . .I'm just. . .scared." Jennifer tripped, catching herself with Freddi's help.

Freddi was now pulling her down the muddy incline, supporting her with one arm while shoving tree branches out of their way with the other. "Come on, let's get to the car."

"But Abby—"

"Abby's at the cafeteria," Freddi grated, her breath coming in quick spurts as they scurried the last few yards down the hillside.

The back of Mitch's cabin came into view, and Jennifer gasped with relief. Both women surged forward, breaking out of the trees and racing across the gravel as fast as they could.

Freddi pulled her keys from her coat pocket, hurriedly unlocking the door on the passenger's side and helping Jennifer into the car. Jennifer reached across the seat to unlock the other door, and Freddi jumped in behind the steering wheel. Throwing the switch on the automatic door lock, she turned to face Jennifer.

Her eyes were hard as they scanned Jennifer's face, then her hands. "You're bleeding," she said shortly.

Dazed, Jennifer glanced down at her hands. Lifting them palms up, she stared at them dully.

Opening the glove compartment, Freddi found a light-colored scarf and wrapped it around Jennifer's hands. "Keep that on until we get to the campus."

She punched the key into the ignition. Waiting only an instant for the powerful engine to roar to life, she shifted hard into reverse and skidded out of the driveway, throwing gravel as she careened onto the road.

In spite of the blistering pain now radiating from her hands, Jennifer felt her mind begin to clear. "Abby's all right?" she asked, looking over at Freddi.

"She's fine. I talked with Mitch. Apparently someone called while we were in town and asked her to come back to the cafeteria and help with desserts for tonight. Mitch drove up to get her but didn't think to leave a note."

"How did you know where to find me?"

"I didn't," Freddi said, keeping her eyes on the road. "I drove down to tell you about Abby after I talked with Mitch, and when I couldn't find you I came around back and just started walking. I saw footprints a couple of places, and some of them were too big to be yours; I got worried. Then I heard you running and tried to follow the sound." Glancing over at Jennifer, she asked, "What happened?"

The heater began to purr with warm air, and little by little the constriction in Jennifer's chest loosened. Huddling forward on the seat, she drew in a deep breath—her first for what seemed like hours—and started to describe the harrowing events of the last half hour to Freddi.

The entire time she talked, she kept her eyes shut. She had seen enough of the mountain for one day.

11

He'd been watching the teacher's cabin for over an hour. Slouched down behind the steering wheel of the van, which he'd parked in a dense grove of trees several yards below the cabin, he was far enough away that no one else would see him—but close enough that he could see anyone entering or leaving.

They were all inside now. The old diz had showed up with the good-looking woman in the Benz no more than five minutes ago. If the routine was the same as the night before, they'd leave for the campus in another hour or so.

He was still trying to figure the connection with the dark-haired dish and the old lady. According to the program he'd picked up, she was some big-deal writer from Chicago. Back in her hometown to do a workshop. So why was she playing roomies with the old woman?

He was beginning to wonder just how much squawking the old crazy had done. One thing sure, he was going to up his price when he got back. In the beginning he'd hired on for three hits, tops. A week ago he'd thought he had it down to one—the old woman. Now it looked like he still had to take care of her plus at least four others—the teacher, the writer, the blind man, and his snoopy wife.

What was her name—it was on the program—*Kaine. Jennifer Kaine.* Did she know he'd seen her this afternoon, up there in the woods?

He grinned, his eyes still fastened on the cabin. He could have offed her right there in the clearing if he'd wanted to. Dumb broad left herself wide open. He could have snapped that scrawny neck of hers with one hand. He didn't need a piece to take care of the likes of her.

But that wasn't in his plan. He had no intention of leaving any bodies behind. The only thing that mattered was that no one would have doubts that the old woman was dead.

No problem with that. All that was left now was to get the job done and get out. He'd messed around long enough with these hicks.

Fast and easy, that's how it was going to be. He wasn't about to waste time taking them out one-by-one. All he needed was the right time and a can of gasoline.

Five people, one cabin, one fire. Piece of cake. No, make that *four* people. He had other plans for *Gwynevere*.

He shook his head, grinning. Even her name was classy.

He looked at his watch. Almost six-fifteen.

When he glanced back to the front of the cabin, he saw the door open and the teacher walk out on to the deck with the writer. They talked for a minute—Donovan looked mad about something—then they walked the rest of the way out to the driveway, ignoring the light rain.

The teacher opened the door of his pickup and reached inside for something, then turned and handed what looked like a letter to the woman. They fussed at each other a few more minutes, then the woman got in the Mercedes and backed out.

Catchside waited until the teacher went back inside the cabin before starting the van and pulling out.

He stayed a safe distance behind the Benz all the way down the mountain. When she reached the intersection to the highway, instead of turning right and heading toward the campus, she turned left.

Where was she going?

He sat at the intersection long enough for a couple of other cars to get between him and the Benz, then pulled out and started down the highway after her.

Wherever she was going, she was alone. That's all he

needed to know.

Staying behind the red Caprice and the Toyota, he continued to keep the Benz in view. This stretch of road was straight and level enough that he could keep her in sight with no problem.

About a mile up, the Toyota turned off onto a dirt road, leaving only the Caprice between him and the Mercedes. He eased up on the gas pedal a little, at the same time turning his wiper blades on high to keep up with the rain, now coming down harder than ever.

Just ahead of the Caprice two kids on bicycles bumped onto the road from a driveway. Both of them were pocketed in yellow rain slickers with hoods and carrying newspapers in their bike baskets. They edged far enough into the right lane that the Caprice had to pull back fast, cutting his speed by half.

With an ugly growl of anger, Catchside tapped his brake. The Benz was already out of his view. Hunching forward over the wheel, he jammed the accelerator to the floor and leaped left, tearing around the Caprice and the bikers, throwing water several feet into the air as he flew by.

As soon as he passed, he whipped the van back to the right lane. Glancing in the rearview mirror, he saw one of the bicycles hit the berm and its rider go flying off into the ditch. An instant later the other kid crashed off the road right behind him.

He shrugged when he saw the Caprice leave the highway and pull in behind the kids.

Good for you, jerk. You and the little creeps can all get drenched together.

He could see her again, about three-quarters of a mile ahead. She went past the turnoff to the dam, her speed was holding steady. Then her right turn signal came on, and she pulled off the highway.

Resisting the impulse to speed ahead and turn off behind

her, Catchside stayed on the road, slowing as he passed the dirt road onto which she'd turned.

The road marker said *Tridale Lane.* Beneath it, on the same pole, a square brown-and-white sign read *Leigh-Hi Farm.*

Catchside pulled his black cap down an inch lower over his forehead and kept on going.

12

All the way out to the farm, Freddi had been torn between a simmering irritation and a swelling sense of dread.

The irritation was targeted at Mitch who, upon learning of her intention to spend the evening alone at the farm, had begun to rail at her about her obstinacy.

Not waiting until they were outside, he'd started to harangue her in front of the still shaken Jennifer, while Daniel and Abby listened with obvious discomfort.

"You're just as hardheaded as you ever were," he had declared. "I'd think that after what happened to Jennifer this afternoon, you'd use a little judgment."

At that point, Freddi had said a hurried good-bye to the others and pushed past him, right on out the door.

Following her, he'd insisted, "There's nothing out there that won't wait until I can go with you."

"I don't *need* you to go with me, Mitch." Inordinately pleased by his concern, yet annoyed by his overbearing attitude, she'd added, "I'll be back at Abby's by eight, eight-thirty at the latest."

Ignoring her attempt to placate him, he'd ended his tirade with the observation that sometimes she didn't show a "lick of sense."

If she hadn't been so exasperated with him, Freddi now thought, smiling to herself, it might have been almost amusing. She had managed to curb her own temper, waiting until he'd finished grumbling before sweetly requesting the fax report he'd brought with him from the campus. Mitch's parting shot as he'd smacked the report into her hand had been something about her possessing "all the common sense of a grapefruit."

111

Oddly enough, the confrontation had seemed to melt at least one of the several layers of ice between them. Perhaps, Freddi thought, still smiling, because it had brought things back to a more normal state of affairs. Conflict was familiar territory for the two of them.

As for the expanding ball of dread in her midsection, she was sure she owed it all to Monster Man. She was just as certain it was only going to get worse once she opened that report from Henderson.

Henderson, whose mood swings ranged from cynical to glum depending on the time of day, had been predictably morose throughout their telephone conversation that morning. Before hanging up he'd warned her that any stranger fitting the description of her "monolith in black" would assuredly fall into one of three possible categories: sociopath, psychopath, or lunatic.

"I'd opt for *lunatic*, seeing as how he has nothing more to do than smack around the woods in the rain," had been his parting shot after promising a fast but thorough report.

Freddi's mind had been working overtime ever since Abby had described her recurring dream early that morning. Her writer's imagination insisted on outlining a number of possible scenarios, all of them chilling.

That someone was stalking Abby she had no doubt. Obviously Monster Man had been watching Abby's cabin—and Mitch's. She knew, without knowing *how* she knew, that Mitch, and possibly anyone else associated with Abby, was in danger.

The question was *why*? Why would he be dogging the seemingly innocent, obviously harmless Abby? What was he doing lurking in the Ridge woods like some medieval forest creature? Was he the one responsible for the savage rifling of Abby's cabin and the senseless slaying of the cat?

And then there was Abby's dream. Abby's *nightmare*. She shuddered as she recalled the way Abby had screamed, then clung so desperately to her while describing the "dark water . . .and blood. . .and a man with a gun and no eyes."

What could have happened in that poor confused woman's past to spawn such images of horror?

Questions. So many questions and not an answer among them, she thought with a sigh, reaching to turn up the fan on the car's heater.

Approaching the turnoff to the farm, she shot a cursory glance in the rearview mirror, frowning with unease when she thought she saw a dark van in the distance behind her. Flustered, she kept her eyes riveted on the mirror while switching on her turn signal.

Pulling off the highway onto the narrow dirt road that led to the farm, she deliberately slowed the Mercedes to a crawl, while keeping her gaze fixed on the rearview mirror. After a couple of minutes she drew a long breath of relief. The black van passed the turnoff and went on up the highway without so much as slowing down.

Pressing the accelerator, she gave her white-faced reflection in the mirror a sheepish grin. *Black-van paranoia, Gwynevere? There are probably only a hundred or more cruising around the county.*

With a shake of her head, she started watching for the familiar blue and white buildings that patched most of the entire right side of Tridale Lane like a checkerboard, the buildings that made up Leigh-Hi Farm.

Home.

For the first half-hour inside, Freddi found herself unable to do anything more than walk through the restored nineteenth century farmhouse—looking, touching, remembering.

Even though she'd spent several hours here on her first day back, the same bittersweet waves of memory had again rolled over her full force tonight, almost as soon as she'd stepped out of the car.

Now she was in her old bedroom, sitting in the middle of the bed, her legs tucked snugly beneath her. Strange, how the brick-walled room still seemed to hold the same cozy warmth that had blanketed her with security throughout all her growing-up years. As it had been then, the cherry four-poster was covered with the Kentucky Rose quilt her grandmother had made before Freddi had ever been born. Both front windows were covered with prim Cape Cods—obviously freshly laundered by Mrs. Kraker. Even the toddler-sized carousel horse carved for her by her Great-Uncle Robert stood in its usual place by the door, wearing its same blue saddle and gold harness.

Freddi had been unprepared for her reaction to the house, in particular to this room, which had served as playroom, hideaway, and retreat. Here she had grown from girl to woman, and the walls seemed to echo with her carefree, childish pranks, her girlhood dreams, her tears, her laughter, and her longings.

She felt suddenly weary and recognized the signs of emotional fatigue rather than physical. Could she really live here, alone, in this rambling old barn of a house, beloved as it was to her? Or was she merely playing a game, acting out the fantasy she'd been having for the past few months? Should she have come back at all?

And Mitch. How did he really feel about her being here? Until that awful first meeting, it hadn't occurred to her that he might resent her coming back. She had hoped for at least a hint of welcome, even while she'd feared his indifference; what she hadn't anticipated was his barely concealed hostility.

She thought she might have been able to deal with indifference, but the resentment, the bitterness she'd seen behind his carefully impassive gaze was breaking her heart.

114

And yet there had been moments—few, admittedly—when she thought she'd glimpsed something else, some fleeting, elusive wisp of a remembered smile in his eyes, a glint of fondness. Or had she only imagined it because she longed so desperately for some small sign of affection?

Questions with no answers. She sighed, then stretched, uncoiling her legs and swinging her feet over the side of the bed. It seemed the only thing she could be reasonably certain of at present was the condition of the river. Before driving back into town tonight, she planned to make a run by the lower bank that edged almost the entire north side of the farm. She already knew what she'd find: the river had to be close to overflowing its banks.

Freddi figured they had had at least six or seven inches of rain by now, and if it didn't stop soon, the Derry would surely reach crest by tomorrow. The dam worried her even more. Twice it had given way, and despite reinforcements and governmental assurances to the contrary, her grandfather had maintained it would let go again unless someone found a way to rechannel some of the spring floodwaters into separate tributaries.

Like most natives of the area, Freddi had lived around the river too long to get panicky every time they had a hard rain. But this was more than a hard rain, and she felt increasingly uneasy about it.

So why are you sitting here doing nothing, Gwynevere? Let's get the family treasures moved to higher ground.

Pushing herself off the bed, she went downstairs and started to work. After nearly an hour of searching through cabinets and cupboards, she had several stacks of photograph albums, scrapbooks, boxes of her grandmother's needlework, and miscellaneous other keepsakes piled up in the middle of the hall, ready to be carried upstairs.

Scooping up a hefty load of albums and scrapbooks into

her arms, she went up the steps and down the hall. There were four bedrooms on the second floor, one of which had never been used for anything other than storage. It was this room she planned to use now.

The door was open, but the room was dark. With her elbow, she flipped the light switch and stepped inside, making a face at the damp, musty smell that greeted her.

The room was unfurnished except for an old daybed, her grandmother's treadle sewing machine, and some boxes. Freddi unloaded the albums on top of the daybed, pushing them flush to the wall so they wouldn't topple over. Then, leaving the light on, she went back downstairs for more.

She was almost to the top of the steps on her second trip, her arms again full, when the lights went out, plunging the house into total darkness.

Stunned, she teetered on the step, reeling from the sudden loss of vision and the burden in her arms. She felt a split second of panic and uttered a small sound of despair. With her arms full and nothing surrounding her but a wall of darkness, she was afraid she was going to lose her balance and pitch backward down the steps.

Trembling, she leaned against the banister, then carefully shifted the box of needlework and scrapbooks from her arms to the top step. Slowly, she started back downstairs, feeling along the wall with one hand, gripping the banister with the other.

It was probably the rain. The wind was up; it had been rattling the windowpanes for the last hour. Then, too, the house hadn't been occupied for over two years; there was no telling what condition the wiring might be in. Power outages were common throughout the county, especially in the valley during a heavy rainstorm.

She stood unmoving at the bottom of the steps for another moment, then turned and started for the kitchen to find a flashlight. Feeling her way along the wainscoted walls of the hallway, Freddi reminded herself to stay calm.

The wind chose that moment to hurl a strong burst of rain against the windows. Startled, Freddi tripped, stopping and clinging to the wall for a few seconds.

The vicious hail of rain on the roof and the groaning blasts of wind around the house made it difficult, nearly impossible, to hear anything else. But she heard *something*, a sound her mind now scrambled to identify.

There. She froze, listening. From the back of the house—the kitchen—she heard it again. Louder this time. A rattling, then a thud.

Scarcely breathing, Freddi put her hand to the swinging door that opened onto the kitchen, waiting.

Somebody was trying to force the back door.

Her stomach knotted, and her pulse lunged. *Wait,* she cautioned herself. *Just . .wait.*

She dropped her hand away from the door, clenching it and unclenching it at her side as she tried to draw a deep breath. A sudden howl of wind seized the house. Freddi jumped, balling a fist to her mouth to keep from crying out. Cautiously, she put her ear to the door, trying to hear what was happening on the other side.

Both the front and back doors were steel, she reminded herself—steel and equipped with deadbolts and security chains. The back door had even been braced with a chair shoved under the knob—Mrs. Kraker's doing, she felt sure. She knew for a fact the doors and windows were all locked; she'd checked them earlier, when she first arrived at the house.

Holding her breath, she listened for a few more seconds, but heard nothing more.

Move, will you? Find a flashlight. That door's a veritable fortress . . . you'd have heard a lot more racket than you did if anyone had broken through.

Expelling a sharp breath, she gingerly tested the swinging door, pushing it forward inch by inch, finally stepping into the kitchen, then waiting. She could see nothing. The room was black and silent.

Freddi moved cautiously across the floor, feeling her way past the refrigerator, the electric range, then on to the sink. Fumbling for the drawers beside the sink, she opened the second one on the right, blindly searching its contents. Nothing but silverware. She tried the one beside it, tugging at it a couple of times before the swollen wood finally let go with a screech.

She jumped, then froze, waiting in the darkness to see if she'd been heard. No sound came from the door, so she rummaged through numerous unidentifiable items, finally discovering a box of safety matches. Not as good as a flashlight, but better than nothing.

She tried one more drawer. As soon as she opened it, her hand closed over a full-sized flashlight. Now, if only the batteries were still good.

They were. Aiming the beam of light at the floor, and shading it with her other hand, Freddi started across the room, hovering close to the wall until she neared the window. Killing the light, she nudged the curtain slightly to one side and looked out.

Nothing. Nothing but rain and darkness.

With the light still out, she moved to the back door to listen.

Again nothing. Not a sound.

Satisfied, Gwynevere? It was only the wind that had you shaking in your socks, kid.

Only the wind. Then why was her heart still banging away at her throat?

Because it wasn't just the wind, and you know it. . . somebody was at that door.

Somebody? Could just as easily have been a wet pooch

118

looking for a dry bunk, right?

She turned the flashlight on just long enough to glance at the face of her watch, astonished to find that it was almost nine-thirty.

Dousing the light, she realized that, at the moment, all she wanted to do was get out of the house and go back to Abby's cabin. Mitch wasn't likely to waste any energy fretting because she wasn't home yet, but Abby and Jennifer might be. She'd deal with the rest of the stuff in the hall tomorrow; hopefully the power would be restored by then.

Do you really want to go outside? There's no light out there either, you know. . .no yard light, no moon, no stars.

Disgusted, she gave herself a mental shaking. She was *going*, and that was that. It was late, she was tired, and she still hadn't even glanced at Henderson's report. She'd go back to Abby's, have a hot shower and a hot cup of cocoa, in that order, and then find out what Henderson had dug up for her.

Unwilling to analyze her growing urgency to leave the house, she switched on the flashlight and started across the kitchen, snatching her purse from the end of the counter, where she'd tossed it earlier. Glancing in the side pocket to make sure the fax report was still there, she headed toward the door off the kitchen. She'd grab her raincoat from the hall closet and get out of here.

She was only inches away from the swinging door when she heard a muffled thud at the front of the house.

She tensed, moving closer to the door. For a long moment the only sound in the room was her heartbeat flailing her chest. Suddenly she heard a sharp popping sound, then silence.

The front door.

She caught a breath, held it as her mind groped to identify what she'd heard.

119

A gun?

A gun with a silencer. Her blood froze and her heart leaped to her throat. Her legs suddenly felt as if a magnetic field were sucking them into the floor. She saw the ball of light at her feet start to break up and realized that her hand was trembling almost uncontrollably. A hood of cold, dark panic slipped down over her head and clutched at her throat, forcing her to gasp for breath.

The image of an immense, dark-clad figure standing on the rise across from the campus flash-froze on her mind, and something close to raw terror richocheted through her body.

He was in the house.

She knew with chilling certainty that she had only seconds to react. Her mind scrambled for focus.

He thinks I'm upstairs.

If he'd been watching the house—and she knew he had—he would have seen the light go on in the spare bedroom shortly before the power blew.

He'll head upstairs. . .I have time. . . .

Suddenly, a firestorm exploded in her stomach. With dismay, she felt the ulcer that had been dormant for nearly a month roar to life. A band of clammy perspiration ribboned her forehead as she gripped the flashlight. With her free hand, she clutched her purse to her stomach, bending nearly double at the unexpected surge of pain.

She knew she couldn't afford to wait out the attack. Keeping the flashlight beam low, she turned and retraced her steps across the kitchen. At the back door, she carefully pried the chair free. Both hands shook violently as she held the flashlight with one and fumbled to release the security chain and the deadbolt with the other.

Outside, Freddi practically hurled herself off the back porch and around the side of the house. Mindless of the rain slashing her face and coatless body, she raced across the saturated yard like a marathon runner.

The raw sore in her stomach radiated a hot, gnawing flame of agony which she did her best to ignore. Out of the corner of her eye she caught a glimpse of a black van parked alongside the house. The pain surged, but she didn't falter, slowing her speed only when she reached the front of the house.

A frantic glance at the front door standing open confirmed her fear: he was inside. It wouldn't take him long to realize that she *wasn't.*

Training the beam of the flashlight on the ground just ahead of her, she fled the yard, heading for the gravel driveway and the Mercedes a few feet ahead.

Balancing the flashlight under her arm, she began to dig frantically for her keys. Finding them, she turned the flashlight on the lock, glanced down—

The front tires were flat. Savagely shredded. Stunned, she gaped at them blankly, then turned to check the back tires.

They, too, had been slashed to ribbons.

The panic that had been bouncing on the edge of her mind surged forward, threatening to overtake her reason. Lightheaded from the pain and mounting horror, she swiveled around, staring at the house and the gaping door.

She mustn't give in to the fear. . .that's exactly what he would expect. . .what he wanted.

Lord, you are my stronghold and my deliverer, my shield, in whom I take refuge. . . .

Forcing a deep, steadying breath, she hesitated only an instant before pushing away from the car. Breaking into the open, she bolted across the field toward the road.

Fear urged her on as she raced across the road, into a wedge of overgrown pastureland that led to the river. She had to avoid the highway; she'd be completely at his mercy if he came after her in the van. Her best chance was to hide in the belt of woods that rimmed the river; she knew them nearly as well as she knew the inside of the house. There, she'd have the advantage and just might be able to lose him.

As she reached the other side of the road, she stopped for only an instant to let her eyes scan the gentle swell of ground that formed a natural ridge above the riverbank. The slope down to the river was thick with underbrush and dense with berry thickets and briers, but she and Mitch had cleared a path one summer to make blackberry picking a little easier on their arms and legs. She hoped it was still there.

Her back to the road, she strained to see if she could spot the path. Suddenly, the roar of an engine exploded out of the night, and she screamed as a blaze of light pinned her in its glare, and the squeal of brakes etched the night.

Blinded by the headlights, stunned by a blast from the horn, Freddi's mind swung out of control. Whipping around, away from the lights, she poised at the top of the bank, ready to leap down the slope.

A car door slammed. She panicked, losing her footing on the mud-slickened incline. Her hands shot out, flailing wildly in search of something to grab, finding nothing but wind and rain.

"Freeddii!"

Arms went around her, yanking her backward and holding her as she screamed into the night, twisting and struggling to break free.

13

Mitch half-carried her across the field to the truck, trying to shelter her beneath his raincoat as they ran. "It's okay, Freddi, it's okay," he reassured her, holding her close to his side. The Ranger's engine was idling fast. Mitch helped her into the seat from the driver's side, and her hands immediately clutched his arm. Her eyes were still wild, glazed with a terror that made his own adrenaline level bounce off the scale. He waited, holding her, letting her hold him.

Finally, he unfastened her hands from their vise-like grip, prying her fingers loose one by one so he could hold her hands. His eyes went from her hair—so wet it was dripping down over the seat—to her clothes, as drenched as her hair. He turned the heater to high.

"What happened?" When she didn't answer, he prompted, "Freddi? Are you hurt?"

She stared at him blankly, then shook her head. "He was in the house. . .he broke into the house. . . ."

He heard the rising note of hysteria in her voice. "Who, Freddi? Who was in the house?"

She was deathly pale, her eyes wide and vacant. Lunging forward, she tightened her hands on his arm. "We have to get out of here! He'll come after me!"

He saw her turn to stare across the road, toward the farmhouse.

"Mitch! Look!"

He turned. There was a flash of light, distorted by the rain-splattered windshield.

Headlights.

A car was pulling away from the house.

He turned back to Freddi.

"Go!" she screamed.

Prying her fingers loose from his arm, he fumbled to lock the seatbelt around her, then slammed the truck into gear. He whipped it around in the middle of the road, shooting dirt and gravel a foot high as he floored the accelerator and took off toward the main highway.

At the intersection he braked hard enough to nearly stand the Ranger on end. Veering left, he roared down the road toward town, tugging his seatbelt over his shoulder and fastening it as he went.

Keeping an eye on the rearview mirror, he pushed the pickup as hard as he dared in the storm. Chunks of mud blotted the road, runoff from the mountain slopes bordering the highway. Wind-driven rain and fog smothered the truck, making it impossible to see more than a few feet ahead.

He glanced over at Freddi. She was still shaking but not quite as violently now, and she looked more alert.

"Freddi? You okay?"

Without answering, she struggled against the confines of the seatbelt to look out the back window. Automatically, Mitch glanced in the rearview mirror.

Nothing but dark road behind them.

Watching the highway, he reached over to hold Freddi's hand. "Hey, kiddo, can you talk to me? What happened?"

Slowly, she dragged her gaze away from the rear window and fixed them on him. Finally, she nodded. Relieved, Mitch saw that her expression had cleared. She still looked scared, but at least the wildness had left her eyes.

"It was him. Monster Man," she said in a choked voice. "The one Jennifer followed this afternoon. He. . .broke into the house. He shot the lock off the front door."

Mitch twisted to look at her.

"He thought I was trapped upstairs."

He squeezed her hand. "Where were you?"

"Downstairs. In the kitchen. The storm had knocked the power out a few minutes before and—"

She stopped, her gaze sweeping the road, first one side, then the other. The highway lamps were on.

He knew what she was thinking. "The power's not out, Freddi."

Her hand gripped his. "He did it," she said woodenly. "I think I knew that. . .I just didn't want to admit it." Turning in the seat, she clutched his arm. "He'll come after us, Mitch. We have to—"

He saw the wavering glow of headlights in the rearview mirror before she did. With a sharp sound of disgust, he withdrew his hand from hers and gripped the steering wheel, watching the mirror and the road at the same time.

Freddi looked at him, then twisted to look out the back window. *"Mitch!"*

"It's okay," he said shortly. "I'll lose him." *Please, Lord.*

The headlights were moving up fast. Too fast. He pushed the accelerator almost to the floor.

"What are we going to do?"

He heard the panic in her voice, and it shook him. It took a lot to rattle Freddi. Just knowing she was scared sharpened his own fear.

The headlights were gaining when he saw the sign for Perkins Road just ahead on the right. He knew what he was going to do.

Toward the crest of the hill a sharp S-curve bent right, then sharply left again; he cut his speed so he wouldn't lose control.

"Mitch—"

"It's okay," he mumbled, almost on top of the turnoff now. Suddenly he switched off his lights, burying the truck in darkness and pounding rain.

"Mitch, what are you *doing?*"

"Taking the scenic route," he said shortly. "Hang on."

He snapped the truck right, hard, shooting off the highway onto Perkins Road.

Keeping his lights off, he bounced down the narrow, pitted

road, praying there were no new killer chuckholes since he'd driven down it last week.

"You can't see where we are!" Freddi cried, her voice pitched with alarm and incredulity.

"And neither can *he.*"

He slowed the Ranger almost to a stop, watching the rearview mirror closely.

Seconds passed. Then, just as he'd hoped, the van roared by, tearing on down the highway. The hunter in search of his prey.

He looked over at Freddi, unable to see her face in the dark. "You okay?"

He heard her catch her breath. "Sure." Her voice held a tremor, but she sounded more like herself. "I haven't had a ride like that since the last time I was in a pickup with you."

"Missed it, have you?"

She was silent for an instant, then, "Are you going to take this cow path all the way into town?"

"That's the idea. Unless you'd rather play tag with your friend in the van."

Ther was a pause. "Can we at least have headlights the rest of the way?"

"If it'll make you feel better."

"The only thing that would make me feel better right now is an armed escort."

"City life has made you soft, girl."

After another moment, he started on down the road, switching on the Ranger's parking lights for the first hundred yards or so before adding the headlights.

When he was sure they were safe, he couldn't resist reminding her of her foolishness. "I *told* you not to come out here alone," he said, staring straight ahead at the one-lane road, eerily distorted in the rain-sheeted haze of the headlights.

He could almost hear her teeth grind. "If it makes you feel

better to say, 'I told you so,' Mitch, then by all means, go ahead."

He didn't answer. She didn't need to know that he'd been absolutely terrified out of his mind all the way out to the farm, thinking something had happened to her. Something awful.

She was silent for a few seconds before asking testily, "What exactly are you doing out here, anyway?"

His face heated with irritation. "I'd say that's fairly obvious. I was trying to save your neck."

"Oh, *really*," she drawled acidly.

His hands tightened on the wheel. He didn't think he'd ever forget the sight of her, standing out there on the rise of the river bank, soaked to her skin, looking like some kind of a cornered wild animal.

Refusing to let her bait him, he muttered, "You said you'd be back by eight-thirty at the latest. I was afraid—you might have had car trouble." He couldn't fight with her. Not now. Inside he was still paralyzed by the thought of what could have happened to her if she hadn't got out of that house. . . .

"What are we going to do?" The sharp edge in her voice made him flinch.

"First, we're going to go to the police." A thought struck him. "What was in that fax report?"

She looked at him blankly. "I haven't even opened it yet. I was going to read it after I got back to Abby's."

He switched on the truck's interior light. "Maybe you'd better check it before we get into town."

She pulled the envelope from her purse and ripped it open. "You're not going to try to talk to Bannon, are you?" she asked, scanning the first page.

He shook his head. "No, there's a new fellow on the force who seems to know his stuff. Tom Robbins. I've talked with him a few times, and I like him. Maybe he'll give us some help." He paused, watching her read. "Anything?"

He wondered if she'd heard him. Her eyes were devouring the report, her mouth partly open in a look of astonishment.

Abruptly, she turned to him. "Mitch—is Abby alone? Is she still at the cabin?"

He looked at her, then shook his head. "No. I took her down to my place before I left; she's with Dan and Jennifer. Why?"

She nodded shortly, turning her attention back to the report. After another moment, she caught a sharp breath.

"Freddi, will you tell me—"

Her head still bent over the report, she waved away his interruption. "In a minute."

He shot an impatient look in the rearview mirror, sinking back against the seat a little when he saw that the road was still dark behind them.

Finally, Freddi looked up. She kept her face set straight ahead for a long moment. Then she turned to him. "Mitch, we can talk with this—Robbins—if you want, but I think we ought to call the state police first."

He swung around to look at her, and she lifted the report in a gesture of explanation. "Henderson was able to ID the photo of Monster Man."

Mitch nodded, waiting.

"His name is Catchside. Floyd Catchside." She paused, then added, "Among other things, he's most likely a contract killer."

He shot her a startled look.

"I told you I sent a photo of Abby, too—"

Again he nodded.

She expelled a long breath. "If Henderson's right," she said tightly, "Abby's the bottom line on an old contract."

He held his breath.

"He's here to kill her, Mitch."

14

Abby hadn't mean't to eavesdrop on their conversation. It was just that it had been impossible *not* to listen, once she'd heard what they were talking about.

Something was wrong, terribly wrong. Mitch and Freddi hadn't come back to the cabin until very late—almost eleven. And when they *did* finally return, they were both so— peculiar. Why, Freddi had been positively *drenched*—and so nervous. And Mitch—she'd never seen him in such a state, pacing the floor, jingling his keys, snapping at poor little Pork Chop. He wasn't a bit like himself, not at all.

And the way he'd insisted that they all stay together, here in his cabin, the rest of the night—as if he were frightened about something.

Abby knew he and Freddi had gone to the police. That was one of the reasons they were so late, Mitch had explained, rather vaguely, that they had talked with a policeman named Robbins, as well as with the state police. Abby was sure there was something else, something he wasn't telling, but of course she didn't ask.

Finally, thinking she might be in the way—young people needed time alone, after all—Abby had said goodnight and come up to the bedroom. *Mitch's* bedroom, where, according to his instructions, she and Freddi were to spend the night, leaving Mitch to the couch in the living room.

Only a moment ago, however, she'd decided to go back downstairs and get Pork Chop. The little cocker had been tagging after her all evening in Mitch's absence, and his antics *did* help to take her mind off Peaches.

She had started to open the bedroom door, then stopped, her attention caught by Freddi's voice. Leaving the door

129

slightly ajar, she stood there, unmoving. Her breath caught in her throat as she heard what Freddi was saying. . .and an entire fireworks of blinding images exploded in her head, hurtling themselves at her with dizzying speed.

"The widow of *Roger* Chase," Freddi said, dropping down onto an enormous quilted pillow in front of the fireplace. "You know—the health resort developer. He and his granddaughter, Melissa, were murdered a few years ago, on his yacht in Virginia, the *Lady A*. The case was never closed." She paused. "Abigail Chase was the main suspect."

Jennifer was bent over the table in front of the couch, where she had just set a tray of steaming mugs of coffee. Straightening, she turned to look at Freddi. "*Abigail* Chase?" she repeated softly.

Freddi nodded, pulling a little at the legs of the warm-up suit Jennifer had loaned her. "Abigail was Roger's second wife. His first wife died of a heart attack in the late seventies."

From his place on the couch, Daniel leaned over to rub Sunny's ears. "You said Abigail Chase was the primary suspect. Why?"

Freddi reached for the mug of coffee Jennifer handed her, saying, "Because she was the surviving heir after Melissa— Roger's granddaughter. Abigail was on the yacht the day of the murders, too, but she escaped unharmed."

Setting her coffee on the hearth, Freddi went on to explain. "Apparently Chase's only child—Melissa's mother—OD'd on heroine and died when Melissa was still a baby. Roger Chase raised his granddaughter, and he adored the girl. The way his will was set up, if anything were to happen to Melissa, then his wife, Abigail, stood to inherit the entire estate—and apparently it's a *considerable* estate."

Mitch had been standing at the sliding glass doors, his back turned as he stared out into the night. He turned now and came over to the table, smiling his thanks to Jennifer as he lifted a cup of coffee from the tray.

Mitch looked weary, Jennifer thought as she scooted in beside Daniel on the couch and guided his hand to a cup of coffee. Weary and *worried.*

"Was Abigail Chase ever brought to trial?" Daniel asked.

"No," replied Freddi. "There was a hearing, but shortly after it started Abigail's mind apparently just—snapped. The court dismissed the hearing and placed her in a sanitarium for treatment. The estate was tied up from that point on with one legal maneuver after another. Taylor Chase, Roger's brother, tried everything to break the will—he was next in line to inherit after Abigail—but he never got anywhere."

Daniel stopped Freddi before she could go on. "You said Abigail's mind snapped—?"

Freddi began to shuffle pages. "Yes. . .wait, it's further on. Here. According to the newspaper accounts, early in the hearing Abigail became—these are Henderson's words—'extremely agitated, incoherent, and irrational.' It seems that she kept raving about a white-haired stranger." Freddi paused. "A white-haired stranger with no eyes."

"No *eyes?*" Jennifer shuddered at the description. She was beginning to develop a roaring case of jitters. She was also beginning to wish she'd never heard of Derry Ridge. Beside her, Daniel touched her arm as if he'd sensed her uneasiness.

Nodding, Freddi elaborated. "When they took her out of the courtroom for the last time, Abigail was screaming something about her husband and Melissa being murdered by a man with white hair and no eyes. That's all she could remember."

Jennifer put a hand to her throat. *White hair. . .the stranger in the woods had white hair. . .and dark glasses. . . .*

"That brings us to Monster Man." Freddi's voice was laced

131

with disgust. "Henderson gave me a positive make on him. His name is Floyd Catchside. He's thought to be a hired assassin—very professional, very ruthless, and *very* weird. Unfortunately, he seems to be as elusive as he is dangerous. He was court-martialed for some kind of mess in 'Nam but got out of it. Henderson said he bounced around Central America for a couple of years as a mercenary. Off and on he's done some drug running. You name it. If it's illegal, this creep's done it." Her eyes darkened. "But his specialty," she said grimly, "seems to be murder—contract killings. And from what Henderson has been able to learn, he thoroughly enjoys his work. He's also smart enough never to have been positively linked to any of his handiwork."

"Sounds like a real animal." Mitch's voice was as hard as his eyes.

"The worst kind," Freddi agreed. "Incidentally, Catchside is an albino. White hair, pale eyes. He has some vision problems—and several allergies. For reasons of his own," she said, glancing up from the report, "he always wears black."

A heavy net of tension stretched over the room, and Jennifer suddenly felt extremely cold. "Then he's the one Abigail Chase was talking about—the one who killed her family."

Freddi dropped the report into her lap, nodding. "He's also the man in Abby's nightmare," she said. Wiping a hand across her eyes in a gesture of fatigue, she described Abby's dream in detail.

"Freddi—" Daniel was hunched forward on the couch, his elbows braced on his legs, his hands hitched together to support his chin. "Is there any doubt whatsoever that Abby *is* Abigail Chase?"

"None, Daniel. Henderson made a positive ID from the photo I sent. You'd have to know him. Henderson probably has a complete mental file on every unsolved murder in the country over the past twenty years. The guy's a walking data base." She took a deep breath, then blew it out. "Anyway, he said Abigail Chase walked away from a sanitarium in Virginia early last fall and just—disappeared. There was a search, of course, but she was never found."

"That would have been about the time that Abby showed up here," Mitch put in.

Daniel leaned back and crossed his arms over his chest. "So . . . if Abby is really Abigail Chase, and if Catchside is the one who killed her family, then there isn't any question as to why he's here, is there?"

"That's right," Freddi said quickly. "As long as she's alive, there's always the chance she might recover—"

"—and cause a whole lot of trouble for whoever murdered her family—or whoever had it *done*," Daniel finished for her. "Any ideas on who that might be?"

"Roger's brother," Freddi answered without the slightest hesitation. "Taylor Chase. Henderson checked on the will. Taylor is next in line to inherit the estate if both Roger's granddaughter and Abigail are deceased. But," she pointed out with a meaningful look, "the fact that Abigail is missing doesn't constitute a legal death. The estate could be tied up for years unless Taylor can prove that she's dead."

"I don't understand how she managed to get off that yacht alive," Jennifer said.

"She went overboard," said Freddi. "The Coast Guard picked her up a couple of hours later. Apparently her husband must have lived long enough to get off a Mayday. Anyway, Abigail was critically ill with pneumonia for weeks afterward; that's one of the reasons the hearing was delayed."

"And there was no sign of this. . .Catchside. . .when they rescued her?" Daniel asked.

"None. It was as if he didn't exist. That's why no one would believe Abigail's story. I figure he probably had a boat waiting for him—someone dropped him off and picked him up."

"How do you suppose Abby made her way *here* from Virginia? And why has it taken so long for this—Catchside—to find her?" Jennifer asked.

"Sometimes it's the people who aren't really *trying* to disappear who actually have the most success with it," Freddi replied quickly. "Their movements are so competely unplanned that it's next to impossible to trace them. A real pro can almost always track down a person who's predictable, but Abby probably just walked off the grounds and kept right on moving. No logic, no destination, no predictable pattern."

"Psychogenic fugue," Daniel said thoughtfully.

Freddi looked at him. "That has something to do with amnesia, doesn't it?"

Daniel nodded. "People suffering from certain kinds of amnesia sometimes just—disappear. They wander off, start new lives—nobody really knows what motivates them. In Abby's case, even though she can't remember events prior to the trauma that brought on the amnesia, she probably has some degree of residual memory—that's a type of subconscious record of whatever happened to her. She may have wandered away from the sanitarium because she was unknowingly looking for something—or some*one*."

"We *do* know she came here on a bus," Mitch offered. "She'd been in Ashland and Huntington—she remembered the names of those two cities, but nothing much before that."

"There's something I don't understand," Jennifer said abruptly. "If *Abby* is the reason for this—Catchside—being here, then why did he show up at Freddi's farm tonight? Why did he terrorize *Freddi* when Abby's the one he's after?"

It was Freddi who finally broke the long silence that fell on the room. "I'm afraid we're all targets now, Jennifer. Think of Catchside as a kind of computerized missile—a chase-and-

134

destroy weapon. Abigail Chase is his target, and he's going to go straight for her, eliminating any obstacles or risk factors that get in his way. For all he knows, Abby may have remembered what happened that day on the yacht and confided it to one—or all—of us." She stopped, then added, "We're probably in as much danger as Abby is, just because we're a part of her life."

"Mitch in particular," Daniel said quietly.

There was another long silence. "That's right," Freddi agreed heavily. "Mitch in particular."

"What can we do?" Jennifer asked, instinctively moving a little closer to Daniel.

"The state police are going to give us as much help as they can," Mitch replied. "They've already put out an APB on Catchside. And Tom Robbins—he's new on the city police force—jumped right in, too. He promised to make extra runs by both cabins and patrol the Ridge as closely as possible. Meanwhile"—he paused, making eye contact with each of them for a moment before going on—"we all stay together. Freddi had a close call tonight. I think we'll find more safety in numbers."

Abby stepped back inside the bedroom, closing the door as quietly as possible.

The room seemed to sway around her. Her vision blurred, and she reached for the edge of the bureau, clutching at it with a trembling hand. Hysteria surged in her blood, rose in her throat, and she pressed the back of her free hand to her mouth to keep from screaming. Her mind went racing backward, tumbling out of control down the dark, slippery corridor to the past. . . .

Roger. . .and Missa. . .

Dead. Both of them, dead. . .on the yacht.

She had been below deck, starting up the stairs. . .she'd heard Missa's panicky screams, began to run. . .she saw

135

Roger first, struggling with an enormous man in black clothing, a mammoth hulk of a man wearing dark glasses. . . and holding a gun.

Her own screams had drowned out Missa's. . .the big man's head swung around, long enough for Roger to force the hand with the gun backward. . .the man staggered, then righted himself, aimed the gun at Roger.

Missa threw herself in front of her grandfather. . .there were shots. . .Missa fell first, then Roger.

He cried out as he fell. . ."*Get off the boat, Abby! Jump, Abby. . .jump!*"

The man turned toward Abby, leveled the gun. . .she flew at him, screaming, pounding at him. . .he was like a wall of granite. . .she clawed at his eyes, knocked the dark glasses off as she raked her nails across his face. . .he'd slung a hand over his eyes to shield them, then lowered the hand to strike her.

But his eyes. . .they were like nothing she'd ever seen. . . nightmare eyes. . .pale, glazed. . .evil stared out at her from some vast, unfathomable chamber.

She saw Roger move. . .he was still alive. . .she made the decision to go overboard, to lure the mad giant away from Roger and Missa, to give them a chance. . .at least a chance.

The man had hesitated a moment before diving in after her. . .the water was cold. . .so cold and so dark. . . . She went underneath the yacht as he circled above her. . .she moved, grabbing air whenever she could. . .he seemed awkward in the water, clumsy and disoriented.

Using what little strength she had left, she began to swim out, away from the *Lady A*, staying below the water as much as possible, putting distance between them.

But he came after her. . .awkwardly. . .but he was gaining on her, closer. . .closer. . .her arms were lead, her legs had weights on them. . .the water was sucking her down. . .her

136

ears were pounding, her heart hammering. . .she fought to go on. . .pushed her head above water.

There was a noise. . .a loud churning, like the sound of an engine.

Then nothing. . .nothing but dark water.

Abby opened her mouth to scream, but the only sound that came out was a soft cry of despair. Slowly, blankly, she looked around the room.

The dark water was gone. But Catchside was back.

This wasn't the first time she'd remembered. . .things. Sometimes, in the middle of the day while she was working in the cafeteria or cleaning for Mitch, a puzzle would form in her mind and something would start to nudge a piece into place, close enough that she could almost feel her memory touching it. But then it would slip away, disappearing before she could fit it back where it belonged.

Now the pieces were all coming together at once, and it was too much, too fast.

Abby began to cry. She cried as she had never cried before. Tears boiled up in her throat, spilled from her eyes, poured down her face. Tears for the family she'd loved and lost, for the time that had been torn away from her. Tears of remembered grief—and renewed dread.

15

"Daniel, is Abby going to be all right?" Jennifer whispered in the darkness of the bedroom.

Still dressed, Daniel sat on the side of the bed, absently stroking Sunny's head. "I think so. She'll have to have some professional help for awhile, but once she comes through the shock of getting her memory back, I believe she'll handle the rest all right."

Jennifer propped herself up on her pillow, studying his shadowed profile. Seeing him rub a hand down one side of his face in a gesture of fatigue, she reached to touch his arm. "Shouldn't you try to get some sleep? It's almost two."

Shaking his head, he stretched his arms out in front of him, then dropped his hands to his knees. "I just came in to see about you. I've been worried about you all day, after what happened on the hill. Do you think you can sleep now?"

"My scare was nothing compared to Freddi's. I'm all right."

"Okay. I think I'll go back out with Mitch for awhile; he's wired pretty tight right now."

No one was getting any sleep tonight, Jennifer thought wearily. But just after midnight she and Freddi had decided to turn in. When Freddi got upstairs, however, she had found Abby crying her heart out, apparently on the very edge of hysteria.

From then on the focus of everyone's attention had been Abby. Watching him now, Jennifer remembered how good Daniel had been with her. There had been a point at which everyone had been trying a little *too* hard to help the distraught, grieving Abby, with the result that she had grown even more distressed. Daniel had finally stepped in, suggesting in his firm-but-tactful way that perhaps he could help, if Abby wouldn't mind talking alone with him.

He'd stayed with her for well over an hour, soothing her enough that she'd finally drifted off to sleep.

Which was more, Jennifer now thought wearily, than any of the rest of them had managed to do. Sitting up in bed, she hugged her knees to her chest and said thoughtfully, "I don't suppose we can even imagine what it's like for Abby. Not only did she have to endure the horror of seeing her family murdered once, but now it's almost as if she's reliving it *again*." Her heart ached for the small, sweet-natured woman who had so quickly endeared herself to all of them.

"That's probably more accurate than you think," Daniel said. "From what she told me, I got the impression that her memories must be every bit as ugly and as painful as what she witnessed firsthand."

Jennifer rested her head on her propped-up knees. "No wonder her mind blocked it out for so long. Maybe it was the only way she was able to survive the whole ordeal."

"I'm not so sure it was altogether the trauma of the murders that triggered her amnesia," Daniel said, leaning back and bracing himself on one elbow. "I think her feelings of helplessness may have played a part in her memory loss. One of the things that kept coming through as I listened to her tonight was a sense of frustration and deep guilt about what happened on that yacht."

"*Guilt?* But why, Daniel? There was nothing she could have done—"

"But she thinks she *should* have been able to do something," he said, "and that's been gnawing at her subconscious." He turned toward her. "Worse yet, she now believes she's jeopardized someone else she loves—Mitch—and perhaps the rest of us as well."

"Oh, Daniel, I hope you were able to convince her she's wrong."

He was quiet for a long moment. "I tried. But I *understand* those feelings, Jennifer—helplessness, fear, frustration. I'm well acquainted with them myself."

Jennifer touched his arm gently as Daniel continued. "It's going to take more than words to give Abby any real peace. She needs to see an end to the whole nightmare. She needs to feel safe again, and to know that Mitch is safe, too."

Jennifer's mind felt nearly numb with exhaustion, but not so numb she couldn't understand the gravity of their situation. Too weary to feel anything but dismay, she sank back against the headboard and said, "There's no way Abby or Mitch—or any of the rest of us—can possibly feel safe until this. . .madman is stopped." She hesitated, then said, "How *do* we manage to get ourselves into these situations anyway, Daniel? It seems as though every time we leave home, we end up in trouble."

Daniel shrugged and attempted a weak smile. "I suppose it's just a case of being in the right place at the right time."

"I certainly don't see anything *right* about any of this," Jennifer muttered.

"Don't be too sure. The Lord has a way of putting us where He wants us, even if it isn't exactly where we'd like to be. Things may not look so great to us, or even make a lot of sense—but that's because we can't see the entire picture. He can."

Too tired to consider his words, Jennifer simply mouthed a small sound of assent.

He reached for her then, wrapping her snugly in his arms. When she burrowed her head gratefully into the warm strength of his shoulder, he pressed a gentle kiss against her hair.

"Don't worry," he said softly. "We're going to come out of this okay. You'll see."

Jennifer wished she could be as optimistic as he was and wondered if he was even half as confident as he sounded.

She kept her doubts to herself, however, and tried to relax in his arms.

After a moment, Daniel gently brushed his lips across her forehead, then eased her out of his arms and back onto the pillow. "I'll take Sunny out to the living room with me. You get some sleep now."

"You need to rest, too, Daniel—"

"I'll doze in the living room," he said, getting up from the bed and tucking the blanket around her shoulders.

He didn't think she knew what he was up to, but she did. Neither Daniel nor Mitch had any intention of going to sleep, Jennifer realized as she sank down into the pillow. They were standing guard.

The ringing of the telephone was distant but demanding. Squinting into the darkness of the bedroom, Jennifer waited out another three rings before sitting up.

A web of filtered light from the pole lamp outside the cabin laced the room. Glancing at the clock on the nightstand, she almost moaned aloud. It was almost 2:45; she'd been asleep for only a few minutes.

She thought she could hear Mitch talking in the kitchen, then, after another moment, heard him go down the hall toward the living room and yell something upstairs.

Reaching across the bed to the night table, Jennifer turned on the lamp, then swung her feet over the side of the bed and shrugged into her robe.

By the time she walked into the living room, Freddi, still dressed in Jennifer's red warm-up suit, was halfway down the stairs; right behind her came Abby, also dressed but looking slightly dazed. Both Daniel and Mitch were standing in the middle of the room.

She went to Daniel. "What's wrong?" she asked, putting her hand on his arm.

Freddi also started firing questions at Mitch as soon as she

141

cleared the steps. "It's the river, isn't it? Did it go over?"

Mitch nodded grimly. "It's already up about two feet downtown, more in the south end."

Freddi twisted her mouth to one side. "I thought we had till afternoon anyway."

Shaking his head, Mitch replied, "I've got to get down to the campus. They'll start bringing people in soon."

Freddi nodded, turning to Jennifer. "The campus is the main shelter in a flood. It's high enough to be safe. There are only a couple of others—a church in the north end and the high school."

Jennifer felt the first stirring of fear. "Then there *is* going to be a flood?"

Freddi smiled thinly. "That's just a part of springtime in Derry Ridge. But you don't have to worry about it up here, Jennifer. It's the town that takes the worst of it."

Glancing at Abby, Jennifer saw that her usual sweet expression was pinched and frightened, and she was wringing her hands nervously in front of her.

Apparently Mitch, too, had sensed Abby's agitation. Quickly crossing the room, he put a hand to her shoulder, saying, "It's okay, Abby. Remember, I told you what it would be like in case of a flood. We'll be fine."

Abby looked up at him. "How high will the water get, Mitch?"

He shook his head. "There's no way of knowing. But it won't bother us up here."

Turning to Freddi, he said, "That was Tom Robbins who called. The police want everyone who can help to meet at the Student Center. Do you want to go with me?"

"We'll all go," said Daniel. "We can take the Cherokee."

Mitch looked at him, then met Jennifer's eyes over the top of Abby's head. "I...thought maybe the two of you could stay here with Abby," he said uncertainly.

Frowning, Daniel didn't answer right away. Finally, his

142

expression cleared and he lifted his chin a little. "Whatever will help most," he said evenly.

Jennifer swallowed hard at the look of regret on Daniel's face, knowing instinctively that the feelings of helplessness he'd described to her earlier were stirring once again. It was only natural that he'd want to go with Mitch, to take an active part in whatever might be happening in town. Instead, he was being asked to stay here with two women. Just as certainly, she knew he would assume that Mitch had made the suggestion because of his blindness.

It was Freddi's perception and acute sense of timing that turned the situation around. Darting a sharp-eyed glance from Daniel to Mitch, she said bluntly, "I thought you said we should all stay together. Besides, they're going to need all the help they can get at the campus, aren't they?"

Mitch opened his mouth to say something but closed it without uttering a sound when Abby moved a step away from him and said in a surprisingly firm voice, "Freddi is absolutely right, Mitch. Why, I can't just sit up here when there's so much to be done! My goodness, they'll need an enormous amount of food, I'm sure. I should be down there right now."

Jennifer gave Mitch a sidelong glance, unable to stop a smile at the mixture of surprise and uncertainty on his face. "But, Abby, you'll be safer up here," he said. "You won't have to worry about the flood—"

"I won't have to worry about the flood down *there*, either," she announced briskly, leveling an alert, blue-eyed stare at him. "I'll be much too busy. You young people can deal with the flood; I'll help take care of the food."

Jennifer looked at Daniel. Standing with his arms crossed comfortably over his chest, he was grinning openly.

"Abby, you and I *could* use some clothes," Freddi said matter-of-factly. "Why don't you let Daniel and Jennifer take you up to your place in their car and collect some things for

143

both of us? While you're doing that, Mitch and I can go on down to the Center in the truck—we'll all meet there."

As if he were determined not to give anyone a chance to nix Freddi's suggestion, Daniel spoke up. "Sounds good, Freddi. We probably ought to have both vehicles down at the campus anyway. Abby, is that all right with you?"

Abby had already started for the stairs. "I'll only be a minute, Daniel. Just let me get my purse."

Realizing that she was still in her bathrobe, Jennifer, too, started to move. "I can't go *anywhere* until I get dressed." ·

"You're not going to do your hair, are you?" Daniel asked.

She stopped, turning to look at him.

"We may not have forty days and forty nights for this one," he explained soberly.

16

After only fifteen minutes in the crowded Student Center, the low-key headache Freddi had been trying to fend off all night finally burst its confines, spurred on by the turmoil in the lobby.

Both she and Mitch had been put to work as soon as they arrived. A Civil Defense volunteer stopped Mitch in the parking lot. Inside, somebody thrust a clipboard and a pencil into Freddi's hands with vague instructions about the need for a list of the evacuees already on the premises, as well as those yet to come.

Penciling in her most recent entry, she stood near the entrance to the cafeteria, letting her gaze scan the scene in the lobby. The entire Center was a teeming arena of noise and confusion. With evacuation already in process in several parts of town, dozens of families were milling about the building. Crying children tugged at the legs of worried-looking mothers, who in turn were trying to follow the instructions of those in charge. Several tired-looking men with rain-slicked hair and dripping wet jackets paced the length of the lobby, snapping curt orders or clearing obstacles out of the way. The waspish hiss of static from a PTP radio followed a police officer as he threaded his way through the crowd, separating those genuinely needing a place of refuge from idle curiosity seekers taking up badly needed space.

Students and faculty members from the college were hurriedly outfitting one entire wing of the lobby with sleeping bags and blankets. At the opposite end, aluminum tables and chairs had been arranged to serve as an information center for rescue workers and displaced family members.

145

Parting a huddle of teenagers in the middle of the room, Mitch approached. He was still in his rain slicker, and his hair was wet. "Dan and Jennifer haven't shown up with Abby yet, have they?" he asked, his eyes roaming over the room.

Tucking the clipboard under her arm, Freddi shook her head. "They'll probably be another half-hour or more, I imagine, by the time Jennifer changes and they get up to Abby's."

"I just hope Jennifer doesn't have any trouble driving down here," he said. Several spots along the road had been slick with mud on their way in, and twice Mitch had stopped to clear fallen tree limbs and other debris out of the way.

"Have you been outside all this time?" asked Freddi, finally noticing just how soaked he was.

"We were trying to get most of the cars off the parking lot," he answered, carefully slipping out of his dripping raincoat, "in case we need the space later."

Static crackled nearby, heralding the approach of a police officer. It was Tom Robbins. He shot Freddi a quick smile before turning to Mitch. "They tell me you're the man to see for some answers."

"Only if the questions are easy. What do you need?"

"I *need* about six more men and eight hours sleep, but I'll settle for a little reassurance. This is my first time in a flood situation. Are we dealing with anything major here?"

Mitch delayed his answer, then nodded. "Anytime you've got a river the size of the Derry spilling over its banks—and a dam that's kept the whole county looking over its shoulder for more than twenty years—I suppose you need to think in terms of something major."

"I was hoping you'd tell me not to worry," said Robbins, raking a hand through his salt-and-pepper hair as his gaze surveyed the congested lobby. "Any idea about how many people may end up here over the next few hours?"

"That depends on how high and how fast the water rises,"

146

Mitch answered. "I can tell you this much: we have only three shelters, and they've never been enough. Last time we had to put tents up outside to handle everybody. We also ended up with a few who were injured and couldn't make it across town to the hospital."

Robbins looked at him with the hint of a grim smile. "I sure feel a lot better about things now that I've talked with you, professor. Maybe I'll look you up again later." He lifted his hand in a parting wave, answering a call on the PTP as he moved through the lobby.

Mitch smiled a little, watching Robbins walk away before turning back to Freddi. "Does that fall under the heading of creative writing?" he asked, inclining his head toward the clipboard.

"It's as creative as I'm going to get for awhile. Do you suppose they have coffee made yet?" she asked, turning toward the cafeteria.

"Should have. I'd rather wait for some of Abby's, but I'm cold and wet enough to drink just about anything hot. Let me get rid of this raincoat, and we'll see—"

He broke off and he and Freddi whirled around as the shriek of a police whistle pierced the din in the lobby. Tom Robbins yelled for quiet, reaching to yank up the volume on a nearby portable radio before turning to roar out another command for silence in the room. Within seconds, even the children had quieted enough that the radio announcer could be heard.

"*This is a special bulletin for Derry Ridge and surrounding areas:* Waters of the Derry River and Vision Lake are rising at the rate of almost a foot an hour. Both the Derry, already at 43 feet, and Vision Lake, now at 31 feet, are overflowing their banks. Worsening the problem is the fact that the Ryder Bridge collapsed only moments ago, jamming Vision Lake and causing the water to rise even faster.

"There are reports of smaller bridges out and roads closed throughout the county; residents are being evacuated as quickly as possible in several communities. Anyone residing in a flood watch district is advised to stay tuned for further bulletins and to be prepared for immediate evacuation if necessary.

"In response to the numerous inquiries this station has received regarding the condition of Derry Dam, please be advised that no updated information has been communicated to us by county officials. Attention has focused over recent months on the effectiveness of the existing discharge system, as well as a rumored dishing of the dam at its middle, but to date we are aware of no revised reports on either of these conditions. . . ."

The rest of the announcer's statement was lost, overpowered by the sudden, repeated screaming of a siren. With a sharp clutch of fear, Freddi recognized the sound of the valley's only disaster warning system.

She turned to Mitch, and their eyes met. The only time the siren ever sounded was to alert residents to a life-threatening situation. Both of them were acutely aware that the flood conditions had obviously just been escalated from "potentially dangerous" to disaster level.

The total quiet in the Center was unnatural, sudden, and strangely oppressive. Slowly, almost as if on signal, everyone began to move toward the large, wide windows at the front of the building in an attempt to look outside. It was an orderly procession. *Too* orderly, Freddi thought, her own tension swelling at the sight of so many numb, blank expressions and wooden movements.

It was too dark to see anything, and after a few hushed moments, people began to disperse, a few at a time, wandering aimlessly back into the lobby or the cafeteria.

"Still want that coffee?" Mitch asked, taking her arm.

"Desperately—but I think I'll try to find some milk instead."

The truth was that Freddi was beginning to feel ill. She'd had no dinner before her harrowing experience at the farm, had, in fact, put nothing into her stomach except decaffeinated coffee since lunch.

"I hope Abby gets here before long," she said as they started toward the open doors of the cafeteria. "I could do with some food."

"They surely have some sandwiches made up by now." Mitch looked at her. "That's right, you didn't have any dinner, did—"

He stopped at the sound of his name. From the information center at the end of the lobby, Tom Robbins was holding a telephone handset to his ear with one hand while gesturing for Mitch with the other.

Tossing his raincoat over a box that had been pushed to one side, Mitch started across the room. Freddi followed him, wondering at Robbins's strained expression.

The policeman hung up the phone just as they reached him. His eyes went to Freddi, lingering on her face for an instant before he turned to Mitch and said, "It's the dam. The commissioners say it may not hold."

How strange it was, Freddi thought dimly, to finally hear those words, words she'd grown up dreading, yet half-anticipating over the years. Now that somebody had finally voiced them, they sounded unreal, impossible to grasp.

She looked at Mitch, saw one shoulder lift and fall in a tense jerk. "Who called?"

"Coates. He and one of the county engineers are up at the dam now. He said they've got all the spillways and guards open, but there's debris piling up too fast to clear—it's clogging the main screens and gratings."

"What about an alternate spillway?" asked Mitch tersely.

"Apparently they've already cut one through. Coates said they have men digging another makeshift a few feet away from the breast of the dam, and one more at the west end."

Mitch waited, saying nothing.

"They don't think it will help," Robbins added.

Freddi turned from Mitch to the police officer. "Isn't there anything else they can try?"

Robbins seemed to struggle with his reply. "There *is* one thing. They want to cut through one end of the dam and let part of the water out. It'll divert some of the pressure, and if the dam *does* break, at least the water will go out slower than if it breaks through the middle all at once."

"They're that afraid it won't hold?" Mitch's voice was steady in spite of the fact that his face was ashen.

"That's what it sounds like to me. At this point, I think they're looking for a way to save the town." He stopped, glanced down, then raised his eyes to Freddi. "It would mean that your farm would be completely wiped out, Miss Leigh. They said I should tell you."

For a long moment, his words seemed to ring between them. Certain she must have misunderstood, Freddi stared at him and repeated, "Wiped out?"

Robbins gave a short nod, then looked away from her eyes. "Your place and the entire bottoms area will take the worst of it." When he turned back, he said quietly, "I'm sorry."

Fighting a sudden wave of dizziness, Freddi was vaguely aware that Mitch had moved closer to her side. "Does she have anything to say about this?" he asked sharply, taking her arm.

"I'm afraid not," replied Robbins. "There are other farms involved, too, but the decision has to be made by the county officials."

"It sounds to me as if it's already been made," Mitch snapped.

"Don't, Mitch," Freddi said quickly. "He's right. They have

150

to do whatever will save the town." She looked at him. "And the campus. You know what it will mean if the dam blows all at once. It'll wipe out everything in the valley." Swallowing thickly against the painful lump in her throat, she again faced Robbins. "When?"

"They're starting right away. They hope to cut through within the next hour."

An hour. . .within one hour the only real home she'd ever had—her yesterdays, her history, her roots—would all be lost to her. . . .

"Her car's still out there," Mitch's voice broke into her thoughts.

"It doesn't matter," Freddi said, meaning it. What difference did a car make when her entire past was about to be washed away?

"A Mercedes doesn't matter?" The look Mitch turned on her was both skeptical and incredulous.

"Maybe I could get somebody to drive it in for you, Miss Leigh," Robbins offered.

"The tires are all flat," she told him. "Besides, it's insured and nobody has time to bother with that now. There *are* some other things, though, that I—" She stopped. Turning to Mitch, she said, "I had several photograph albums and some other keepsakes stacked up, ready to store upstairs. Maybe I could still save them if you'd take me—or if you'd let me use your truck."

Mitch looked at her, then turned a questioning glance on Robbins.

The policeman hesitated. "It takes a good fifteen minutes just to drive out there."

Freddi touched Mitch's arm with appeal. "That would still give us at least half-an-hour. It won't take that long. I have everything ready; all we'd have to do is carry it outside."

His eyes went over her face. "Okay. But we go *now*. Right now. You get your things out of my office while I call Abby. If

151

they haven't already left her place, I'm going to tell them to stay put. They'll be better off up there than here, especially with us gone."

Nodding quickly, Freddi looked around for someone to continue the evacuee list she'd begun.

"Is she alone?" Robbins asked abruptly.

"Abby? No, the Kaines are with her," Mitch answered. "Why?"

"You might want to check on the power situation up there. It's out several places in town already. I've got a couple of fellows from the faculty checking the auxiliary generators downstairs, so we can at least keep minimal power here. And, professor"—the policeman's good-natured expression hardened—"you and Miss Leigh need to get going. Don't cut yourselves too close, all right?"

Mitch nodded grimly. "Give that clipboard to one of the Red Cross workers," he told Freddi as he headed toward the phone. "We've got to get out of here."

They were silent during the first few minutes of the ride out to the farm, other than an occasional comment from Mitch about the water that was already creeping across the road in some of the lower places. Freddi limited her responses to a nod or a muttered sound of acknowledgment. The slow-burning fire that had ignited in her stomach earlier was flaring in earnest; she had all she could do to keep from moaning aloud.

Trying to take her mind off the pain, she asked, "Abby *did* promise to stay at the cabin until we get back, didn't she?"

Mitch nodded, whipping the steering wheel sharply right to avoid a large clump of mud near the middle of the road. "I talked with Dan, too. They're going back down to my place and stay there until they hear from us. That way, if the power goes out, they can use my battery generator and still have light. Just to be safe, I asked Tom Robbins to give them a call at my place in half-an-hour or so." He glanced over at her. "You realize, don't you, that Abby will be glad to have you stay with her as long as you want?"

Freddi managed a smile. "Abby's going to want her living room back eventually. I can stay at the Lodge until I find something, I suppose."

"Freddi?"

She looked at him.

"I'm sorry about the farm," he said quietly. "I wasn't sure it would. . .matter all that much to you. But I can see it does."

She turned her face away, unable to deal with the kindness she'd seen in his searching gaze. Longing for the privacy to weep, she instead tried to square her shoulders and inject a note of firmness into her voice. "I suppose I didn't realize myself how much it mattered until now," she answered honestly. "It does hurt. . .a lot. But I'll be all right."

Turning back to the road, he said softly, "You'll always be all right, won't you Freddi." It was more statement than question.

She looked at him, weighing his words. Weakness gripped her, making his features appear hazy for an instant. She'd been lightheaded ever since leaving the campus, caught in the net of pain radiating hotly from her stomach. Wiping a hand over her eyes, she fought for a deep breath. "You could never accept that, could you, Mitch?"

He frowned his lack of understanding.

"You always did resent my—independence—isn't that what you called it? You never really wanted me to be in the least self-sufficient. Why, Mitch?"

He studied her for a long moment, slowing for the turnoff to the farm. "Maybe I was afraid," he said quietly.

She shot him a surprised look. Until now, he had invariably denied the possessiveness responsible for so much conflict between them. "Afraid of *what*?"

"Did it ever occur to you that what you thought was resentment was actually desperation?" he asked evenly, keeping his eyes straight ahead as he started down the muddy, deeply furrowed road. "Maybe I thought the only way I could keep you with me. . .was to make you *need* me."

His unexpectedly candid answer stung her heart.

"All I ever wanted was to be as important to you as you were to me." He suddenly looked very tired—tired and defeated. "But you didn't need me. You didn't need *anyone*. You never did."

She couldn't deny the truth of his accusation. There *had* been a time when she had imagined herself to be just that self-sufficient. Why should he believe it was any different now?

Neither of them spoke again until he parked in front of the house. Cutting the engine, he turned to her. "Tell me something, Freddi," he said quietly. "If I hadn't been so paranoid about losing you—if I hadn't tried so desperately to keep you here—would you still have gone away? Did I *drive* you away?"

"*No!*" she cried softly, leaning across the seat toward him. It was incomprehensible to her that he would blame himself. "No," she emphasized again, sinking weakly back against the seat. "It wasn't you. It was the *writing*."

There was a world of bitterness in his eyes when he nodded and said, "It was *always* the writing, wasn't it, Freddi? Nothing else was ever quite as important to you. You put it first, before everything. Including me."

"Yes," Freddi admitted quietly. "That's exactly what I did. And that's what *you* did with *me*." She squeezed her eyes tightly shut, then opened them. "Oh, Mitch, don't you see? We both made the same mistake. I wrapped all my hopes and dreams and faith in one thing: my writing. But it wasn't big enough. It collapsed under the weight. . .it failed me. And you did the same thing. . .you made *me* your world. . .you

154

built your life around me. But I wasn't big enough either, Mitch. So I failed you."

As he sat there, unmoving and silent, Freddi thought she could sense his anger fading to confusion.

"What I had to face," she said urgently, "is that there isn't anyone or anything that won't eventually fail us, that ultimately nothing is. . .enough. . .except the Lord." Her voice caught, but she went on. "That's one reason I came back, Mitch. I knew I couldn't really start over again until I faced myself as I had been. And until I faced you. . .as I am now."

His head came up. Freddi moved to touch his arm, but something in his eyes stopped her.

She wanted him to reach for her, to hold her. She wanted him to press her head against his shoulder and make the world right again, the way he'd always been able to do when they were younger.

Instead, he pulled away from her. "We don't have time for this," he said woodenly, opening the door of the truck.

Wounded by his rejection, Freddi knew a sense of despair like nothing she'd ever felt before. She had to press her hands against the seat of the truck to keep from flinging herself at him and pleading with him to love her again. She ached to tell him now what he had wanted to hear years ago. . .that she needed him, needed him just as much as he had ever needed her. . .perhaps even more.

The problem was. . .Mitch no longer cared.

17

Furious, Catchside huddled among the trees, watching Donovan and the dishy writer leave the cabin a little before three.

He had been all set to finish up before daylight. He even had the gasoline can stashed beneath a decaying tree stump. Within minutes, he would have been inside the cabin. He had to question the old lady, but he didn't plan to waste much time.

It couldn't have been any neater. The five of them together like that—he would have had the job done and been out of town before dawn. Now he'd have to chase them down again.

What would run them out in such a hurry at three o'clock in the morning?

Glowering under the hood of his poncho, he decided to wait a few more minutes. He jumped when the front door opened again and the old woman came out, followed by the blind man and the guide dog, then his wife.

What was going on?

He inched around the tree, watching as they all piled into the Cherokee and took off up the road, in the direction of the old lady's cabin.

In a rage now, he growled an oath and turned, lumbering back through the woods to retrieve the gas can. He took the hillside with fast, broad steps until he came to the van, hidden behind a dense fringe of pine trees near Donovan's cabin.

Opening the door on the driver's side, he reached across the seat to set the gasoline on the floor, then jumped in behind the wheel.

No more messing around. No more delays. No more killing time in this stinking wet mudhole. If he had to take them out one at a time, he'd do it—but whatever he had to do, he was going to do it *now*.

He rammed the key into the ignition and, as soon as the engine caught, he roared out of the clearing and onto the road.

18

Abby's cabin was quiet, disturbingly quiet. The rain had stopped. Jennifer found its absence almost eerie. There was no pounding on the roof, no rattling of windowpanes, no sheets of water crashing against the siding.

It should have been a relief, but instead, the stillness put her on edge.

It's probably not the silence, dopey. . .more likely, it's exhaustion.

The three of them were at the front door, about to lock up and leave, when darkness suddenly fell over the cabin.

Abby uttered a surprised gasp, and Jennifer groaned aloud, instinctively clutching Daniel's arm. "There goes the power."

Daniel and Sunny stopped, waiting.

"Abby, do you have a flashlight handy?" Jennifer asked, straining to focus her eyes, unable to see anything except shadows. "We may need it to get to the car."

"A flashlight? Yes . . . yes, there's one in my bedroom and another in the kitchen, I think. I'll find one, dear. You stay right here with Daniel."

"Be careful that you don't trip over something," Jennifer cautioned as the older woman started toward the hallway. Still gripping Daniel's arm, she turned back to him. "I'm glad Mitch warned us this might happen."

"We'll be better off at his place, if I can get the generator going. He told me what to do, but you and Abby may have to help a little."

Jennifer fidgeted from one foot to the other. "I hope Mitch and Freddi get back soon."

He didn't answer.

"Daniel?"

"They don't have much choice," he said after a few seconds. "A hole's being cut through the dam to relieve some of the pressure on it. In another hour or so, Freddi's farm will be under several feet of water."

"Oh, *Daniel*—no!" Stunned, Jennifer moved a little closer to him. "Is that why they're going out there? Are they going to try to get her car out?"

"No," Daniel said quietly after a moment. "Mitch said Freddi wanted to get some things out of the house—her grandmother's Bible, photograph albums—souvenirs, mostly."

Somehow it didn't surprise Jennifer to hear that Freddi was more concerned about a few keepsakes than a luxury car. It fit the woman she had come to know and respect this week.

When she didn't answer, his hand covered hers. "They'll be all right. Mitch isn't about to take any chances, not with—"

He broke off when Sunny barked, just as Abby walked up behind them in the hall.

"It's all right, girl," Jennifer reassured her, taking the flashlight from Abby and aiming its beam at the door.

The retriever barked again, straining impatiently at her harness.

"Sunny, what is *wrong* with you?" Jennifer muttered, glancing at the retriever. "I think she has to go, Daniel," she said, opening the door. "Maybe you'd better take her harness off before we—"

She froze. The flashlight shook in her hand, its wavering white orb catching and spraying a huge, black-clad man mounting the steps of the cabin. He was wearing a black cap and some sort of nightmarish goggles. He had a gun leveled directly at them.

Jennifer screamed, and, behind her, Abby cried out

159

weakly. Sunny went rigid, then flew into a rage, barking viciously and roaring like a wild thing. Blocking Daniel with her body, she faced the intruder with the gun.

It was impossible to tell what happened next, whether Daniel's grip on Sunny's harness loosened in the confusion of the moment, or whether the retriever tore herself free. With one powerful lunge she leaped at the man, hitting him hard. She was all over him, clinging to him relentlessly, sinking her teeth into his shoulder.

The man reeled, shouted and fired the gun into the air. The bullet went wild, and Sunny went crazy.

But he was too big and too strong for the small-boned retriever. With the gun still in his hand, he ripped her away from his body, hammering her on top of the head with one large fist. Shouting with rage, he then hurled her out into the yard, where she fell with a thud into the wet grass. She squealed when she hit, then whimpered and lay still.

Daniel lunged forward at the sound, but Jennifer threw herself in front of him, screaming. *"No, Daniel! Stay back!"* She tried to slam the door, but the man's leg shot forward, forcing the door open with one massive, boot-clad foot.

"Inside," he snapped, shoving all of them back as he moved through the door.

Ashen-faced, Daniel stumbled as the man gave him another hard shove. "I've got to get my dog—"

"I said *move*, jerk! The dog's dead!" Reaching across him, the man yanked the flashlight out of Jennifer's hand.

The gun never wavered as he kicked the door shut behind him. Backing all of them into the living room, he trained the flashlight on Abby. His mouth spread into a cold smile, and Jennifer thought she was going to be sick. In the backwash glow from the flashlight, his grinning, goggle-masked face was that of an other-world alien.

Evil. It was strong enough that Jennifer took a step backward.

Inclining his head toward an oil lamp across the room, the man tossed a pack of matches from his shirt pocket to Jennifer. "Light it," he ordered in a gruff, phlegmy voice.

Her hands were shaking so violently she used three matches before she got the wick to catch. When she returned to Daniel and Abby, she found the older woman looking as if she might lose consciousness at any moment.

"Sit down," the giant growled, waving the gun toward the couch. Jennifer took Abby's arm, but found her rigid and resistant.

"I said sit *down!*" he roared again, tossing the flashlight across the room.

Forcing Abby to move, Jennifer pushed her gently onto the couch, then sat down beside her.

Daniel started to follow them, but the man pushed him roughly into a chair by the window. Choking back a cry of dismay, Jennifer half-rose to go to him. The man whirled around, turning the gun on her, and she sank back onto the couch.

Daniel's face was a mask of anger, but he merely gripped the arms of the chair tightly, saying nothing.

The man flung his cap onto a nearby table, then reached to pull the goggles away from his eyes, pushing them up above his forehead.

Abby gasped, and Jennifer clutched her arm. The glow from the oil lamp was too dim to see clearly, but she cringed at the small, pale eyes staring at her. Red-rimmed and moist, they looked. . .diseased. Diseased and empty.

He seemed to fill the room with his enormous, intimidating frame. Daniel was a big man, tall and thickly muscled, but Jennifer could see that this . . . lunatic . . . would top Daniel by several inches and most likely outweighed him by almost a hundred pounds. He was *immense.*

Turning his empty-eyed gaze on Abby, he stared at her for

161

a long, tense moment. "Remember me, Abigail?" he asked in a deceptively soft voice, flashing another ugly, long-toothed grin at her.

For the first time since the man had come upon them, Jennifer saw Abby look directly at him. Slowly lifting her wide, frightened eyes upward, she fastened her gaze on the man's face in a silent look of horror.

He let out a heavy, jarring laugh. "Well, now, you couldn't be expected to remember, could you? I don't exist. I'm just some figment of your imagination. A phantom you invented to take the heat off yourself—isn't that what the newspapers said?"

The macabre smile widened as he lowered the gun slightly. "Well, guess what, Abigail: you didn't dream me up after all. There really *is* a Catchside."

19

Mitch left Freddi alone after they finished packing her things in the truck. He'd been aware of her grieving all the way out to the farm and as they loaded her few memories. He knew she had some good-byes to say, and he thought she needed to be alone to say them.

But it was past time they should be leaving, and he was getting edgy. He was worried about leaving Abby with Dan and Jennifer, in spite of the fact that he'd asked Tom Robbins to check on them. The police had their hands full already; there would be precious little time for anything other than what was happening in town. What if that maniac came looking for Abby? Dan was amazing, but he *was* blind.

Closing the pickup's tailgate, he looked at his watch, then toward the house. He couldn't give her much longer.

Dawn was finally beginning to fight its way over the Ridge, a timid kind of daybreak that seemed reluctant to struggle past the saturated skies. Leaning up against the side of the truck, he stared out over the vast, deeply shadowed farmland.

He had a few of his own good-byes to say to this place. Before he was old enough to hire on at the Lodge, he'd worked part-time here for Freddi's grandfather; the farm was almost as familiar to him as his own place on the mountain. And the memories it held for him were even dearer.

He almost felt that, if he looked long enough, he would see Freddi go racing across the field, her hair tucked under the ever-present baseball cap as she dared him to try to catch her. Or maybe he'd catch a glimpse of her perched on the tire swing in the old maple down by the dairy barn, urging him to push her higher. . .or sitting on the top step of the front porch on a Saturday night, waiting for him to pull up in his truck and take her to town. . . .

He closed his eyes in an effort to shut out the memories, unwillingly exchanging them for the words she'd spoken on the way out here—the words she'd seemed so desperate for him to understand. He couldn't seem to shake them off, to silence them in his head. Somehow the truth of what she had said to him insisted on playing over and over again in his spirit . . .

"*. . . I wrapped up all my hopes and dreams and faith in one thing. . .but it wasn't big enough. . .it failed me. . .and you did the same thing, Mitch. . .you made me your world, you built your life around me. . .but I wasn't big enough either. . .so I failed you. . .what I had to face is that there isn't anyone or anything that won't eventually fail us, that ultimately nothing is. . .enough. . .except the Lord. . . .*"

How was it, he wondered, opening his eyes, that she had been able to accept something he had known but put aside for so long?

For years he had blamed her. Then, for a time, he had hated her—or tried to. Finally, he had enshrined her, turning her into something beyond reality, something only his memories could contain. But always there had been that unspoken, unadmitted awareness that he had somehow distorted the order of things, that he had made her *too* important, that he had placed her where no human being had a right to stand. . .between him and his God.

She had accused him of making her his world, of building his life around her.

And he had. To the exclusion of almost everything else.

She's right, Lord. . .I loved her too much. . .always too much. . .more than you. . .more than life. . .how could she possibly live up to that? How could anyone live up to that?

164

Whatever she had been through—and that she had been through *something* he no longer doubted—had brought her face-to-face with her own. . .*stumbling block*. . .the barrier responsible for the distance between her and the Lord.

Freddi had been *his*. . .obstacle. *Oh, Lord. . .I've spent years blaming her for not being bigger than life. . .when all the time I should have realized that nothing is bigger than life except you.*

After a long, cleansing moment, he pushed himself away from the truck and started for the house. Suddenly anxious to hear for himself what it was that had brought her to this new place in her walk with the Lord, he knew his answers would have to wait until later. Right now they had to get out of here.

When he didn't find her inside he thought he knew where to look. He went around to the back of the house, and, sure enough, she was down at the gazebo.

Another indulgence of her grandfather, the small, white latticework building stood atop a gentle swell of ground facing the Ridge. It had been her playhouse, then her "dream house," as she'd called it. She had gone there to write her stories on summer afternoons. Later the two of them went there to talk and plan their future together.

He wondered if she remembered that the first time he'd ever told her he loved her had been inside that gazebo, in the middle of a spring rainstorm.

As he got closer, he saw that she was leaning forward, both hands pressed palms down on the narrow, scrolled banister. Her back was to him, and for a moment he thought she was ill. His heart lunged, but then he heard her and realized she was praying. He couldn't be sure, but he thought she was also crying.

He hesitated, wondering if he should walk away and leave her alone. Then he took another step toward the gazebo, listening, even though he knew he had no right.

"*. . . I know I told you I'd give it all up, if that's what it takes. . .and I will, Lord—the writing, the career, the farm—everything. . . ."*

His heart started to break. She was hunched over even more now, her thin shoulders—too thin, he realized—heaving slightly with her words.

"*. . . But you understand, don't you, that right now I feel as if I'm being torn to pieces? . . .It isn't the farm, Lord, although losing it will be like losing a piece of my heart. . . but I'll get over that, in time. . .and I know you'll help me put my life back together again eventually. . .I know you will . . . ."*

Mitch felt himself choking on her words as if they were being ripped from his own throat.

"*. . .But I don't think the pain of losing Mitch will ever be over, Lord. . .not really. . .I didn't know it would hurt this much, I didn't think anything could hurt this much. . ."* She faltered, then went on. "*. . .Oh, Lord, he was your gift to me. . . and I think you meant me to be your gift to him. . .but we got things all mixed up and ended up putting the gift before the Giver."*

He squeezed his eyes shut, letting the echo of her words roll over him. Wearily, he rubbed his hands down his face, thinking for a moment, when he felt moisture on his fingertips, that it was rain. Only when he opened his eyes did he realize that the wetness spilling down his cheeks was tears.

He moved now, closing the distance between them, stepping up onto the porch of the gazebo and putting a hand on her shoulder.

For a long moment he didn't think she was even aware of his presence. But, finally, she straightened and turned to face him. His gaze traced the tears down her cheeks: then he touched his fingers to them, blotting them as he searched beyond the pain in her eyes for something else, something

166

he had ached to see throughout all the years between them.

"I'm sorry, Freddi Leigh," he said softly, remembering another lifetime of moments like this, when he'd teased her or hurt her feelings in some foolish, unintentional way. "I didn't mean to make you cry."

Her eyes lifted to his, questioning, seeking.

He trapped her hand in his and tugged at it, drawing her closer. His other hand went to her damp hair, then to her cheek. "When there's time, I want you to tell me the rest of your story."

Her look was puzzled, but when she would have questioned him, he pressed a finger to her lips, stopping her. "I want to be sure I understand what you were trying to tell me on the way out here. All of it. But not now. There's no time. I'm going to ask you just one question, and then we have to leave. Okay?"

She nodded, tilting her head even more as she waited.

Calling forth another memory, he took her by both hands and whispered, "Will you be my girl, Freddi Leigh? For always?"

She went deathly still, searching his eyes. He was aware of her trembling as his hands went to her shoulders. "Will you, Freddi Leigh?" He kissed her, gently, at the corner of her mouth. *It was yesterday again. . . .*

With a small sound, she came into his arms and he kissed her once more, returning his heart to her, asking once more for the gift of her love.

He looked at her, saw her smiling at him through lingering tears. "Say it," he urged, gently stroking her hair, pushing it back from her temples.

"I'll always be your girl, Mitch Donovan. For as long as the river runs, I'll be your girl."

She remembered. . . .

When he kissed her this time, he was promising her what

167

she had just promised him. *Forever. . . .*

Daybreak rose in his heart at the same time it came up over the mountain.

"I wish we'd left sooner," he said worriedly as the pickup bumped onto the dirt road leading away from the farm. "We're cutting it too close."

He went on, talking mostly to himself, trying to give vent to the swell of anxiety that was about to choke him. Freddi was sitting close to him, as she had years before when they were teenagers. He put his arm around her shoulder and pulled her a little closer. He felt better. Just having her back in his life made everything better.

"First thing when we get back to town, we'll get a Civil Defense boat and go up to my place. I want to get Abby and the others out of there, down to the campus where they're not so isolated."

"You think we'll need a boat this soon?"

He turned sharply left to avoid a deep pit in the road. "Probably not," he answered distractedly, straightening the steering wheel. "But I don't want to chance getting stuck on the other side of the Glen."

"You're not worried about the campus?"

He shook his head. "Even if the whole thing blows, the extra spillway will slow it down enough to save the campus. It won't have the momentum to climb that high. It's the town and the bottoms that will take the worst." He paused, then added, "I just hope we did the right thing, leaving them at my place."

When Freddi didn't answer, he looked at her. Frowning, he saw that her face was sickly white; her mouth contorted with pain. She was hugging her midsection with both arms wrapped around her body.

"Freddi? What's wrong?"

She shook her head, saying nothing. Moving away from

168

him, she reached for her purse and began to fumble inside it until she pulled out a small white bottle.

"What's that? Are you sick?"

"I'm all right," she grated between clenched teeth.

He watched her open the bottle and take three deep swallows before replacing the cap. Alarmed now, he asked her again, "What is that stuff? What's it for?"

"It's just. . .Mylanta," she said, adding grudgingly, "I have an ulcer."

Keeping his eyes on the road, he frowned. "An ulcer? Is that serious?"

She uttered a choked sound that sounded like a laugh. "Mitch, you are probably the only person in my entire world who doesn't know all about ulcers."

"I know about ulcers," he said with a trace of defensiveness. "I just don't know how serious they are."

"Mine. . .was better. As long as I avoid junk food binges and stress, I can live with it. I guess I haven't done so well with either this week."

No sooner were the words out of her mouth than she jerked against the seat, moaning softly.

Freeing his hand, Mitch touched her forehead. Her skin was cold, yet clammy with perspiration. "Can I do anything?"

She shook her head weakly.

"Is it always this painful?"

"No. Not always," she said, gritting her teeth.

Watching the road, he skimmed a kiss over the top of her head. "You just need some good old-fashioned country living," he said. "That'll take care of the stress."

"Right. This week has done a lot to eliminate the stress in my life."

"Yeah, well, you'll see. We'll get some weight on you and—"

He broke off, hearing something that sounded like several

loud booms of thunder or a series of explosions.

His eyes went to the rearview mirror and locked on the sight of an enormous wall of water bearing down on the valley.

It took a few seconds for reality to pierce his panic. "Here it comes," he choked out, yanking his arm free to grip the wheel with both hands.

At first it looked like a dark, dense layer of fog rolling in over the valley, treetop high. He reached to crack his window a little so he could hear, jolted by the thundering noise that rolled through the opening.

White-faced, Freddi whipped around. He heard her gasp, felt her clutch his shoulder. "Mitch. . ."

"I know. . .I know. . .just hang on."

He slammed the accelerator to the floor, keeping his eyes on the rearview mirror, watching the horror grow and build behind them. Churning waves of water several stories high pushed shapeless masses of debris in front of it, flinging trees and chunks of earth as if they were nothing.

Reaching the intersection at the main highway, he made a frenzied sweep of all directions, then shot left onto the road.

He tilted the rearview mirror a fraction, watching the wall closing in on them. It had to be moving twenty miles an hour or more, sucking up everything in its path, grinding it up, tossing it out, gaining momentum with every second.

"Are we going to make it?" Freddi's voice next to him was oddly quiet, even steady. She had never been the hysterical type, but he wouldn't have blamed her if she'd opened her mouth and started to scream. He wasn't so sure he was too far from it himself.

"We'll make it," he said tightly, wishing he felt even half as confident as he tried to sound.

Her hand still clung to his shoulder as she again turned to look behind them. He heard her catch a sharp breath before she turned back to study his face.

"We'll make it," he told her again, aware of her fear, nearly choking on his own.

In another quarter mile they would reach the bridge over Job's Trace, the lowest point of the bottoms where the valley began to narrow, then merge and climb upward until it became one with the Ridge. If they got that far, he could outrun the rolling monster behind him.

It was coming down on them fast now, unleashing total destruction on everything in its path. He stabbed again at the accelerator, but it was already glued to the floor.

They were on the downhill run. The valley was flying by, the Ranger skimming air as it ate up the road.

Then he saw the bridge. Or what had been the bridge before the swollen stream had apparently pushed it up and squirted it into the air. There were pieces of steel and concrete strewn on both sides of the road, part of a narrow pillar upended in the roiling water. Nothing else.

Mitch sucked in an enormous gulp of air, gripping the wheel until pain shot through his knuckles.

Beside him, Freddi reared back hard against the seat, her fist stuffed hard against her mouth as if to stifle a scream.

Mitch grabbed one last look in the rearview mirror and knew he had to go for it.

"*Hang on!*"

Giving one mighty rebel yell, he hunched forward over the wheel. The Ranger lifted off, bouncing them up off the seat, throwing them hard against their seatbelts as it leaped across the stream and landed front-end first on the other side. The bumper scraped asphalt for a good two feet until the lighter back end of the pickup finally touched down.

He took the hill full-tilt, swallowing down the taste of raw panic threatening to block his airway.

Fishtailing up the mud-washed hill, Mitch shot a frantic

171

glance at the rearview mirror. The wall of water, like a furious monster whose rampage had been temporarily thwarted, had crested only feet below them and was now surging madly over the fields, gathering new power as it continued on its death route toward the valley.

His heart banging wildly against his chest, he continued their race toward the safety of the campus, knowing with agonizing certainty that the town was only seconds away from destruction.

But Freddi was with him, and they were safe. He couldn't let himself think of anything beyond this moment.

Hoping to reassure her, he said in a woefully unsteady voice, "Didn't I tell you we'd make it?"

When she didn't answer, he looked over to see her draining the upended Mylanta bottle in one continuous gulp.

20

Abby's face was a mask. Catchside had been grilling her for nearly an hour, hammering away at her with a ruthless, relentless cruelty that made Jennifer want to scream at him in rage.

Despite his tenacity, Abby had told him nothing. In fact, so convincing was her blank bewilderment that Jennifer could almost believe she'd somehow been drawn back into the depths of the amnesia. More likely, though, she felt Abby's attempts to mislead her interrogator were motivated by a desire to protect everyone else.

Jennifer no longer believed it would make the slightest difference. With a dreadful certainty, she felt they were all doomed, no matter what they did or didn't know about Abby's past.

By dawn, the intimidating giant was noticeably frustrated. Standing in the middle of the living room, he seemed to fill every inch of open space with a forbidding, malevolent energy. If possible, he was even more menacing in the gray light of morning crowding through the curtains than he had been in the shadowed glow of the oil lamp. Jennifer sensed that the man was little more than a deranged, volatile psychotic whose actions were hopelessly unpredictable. One minute he would be soft-voiced and unnervingly calm, the next, crude and savagely irrational.

Abby's composure under fire astonished her. Other than the repeated pulling of her hands in her lap and the cast of horror in her eyes, she seemed isolated, almost invulnerable to his terrorizing tactics.

"All right, Abigail, if that's the best you've got for me, we might just as well get this over with." He was back to his quiet-voiced calm, which somehow frightened Jennifer even more than his raving.

"It's a real shame about your. . .*amnesia*, Abigail. I was kind of hoping to find out why old Taylor hates your hide the way he does."

When Abby gave him a blank look, he went on, goading her with a mocking smile. "I never did believe it was just the money, not that he isn't a hungry old bird. It occurs to me that maybe it was you who tipped his brother off about the operation Taylor was running on his own."

He watched Abby as if to measure her reaction.

When there was none, he continued to ramble, his tone deceptively low, his words quick and detached. "Yeah, when that righteous hubbie of yours found out about old Taylor using some of his fancy resorts to front a drug operation, that's when he started making noises about changing his will, right?"

With seemingly genuine confusion, Abby merely looked at him.

He glanced at Jennifer, then Daniel. "Say, that's right. If Abigail here is telling the truth about not knowing who she is or anything about her past, that means you don't know either, right?" He grinned. "Well, let me introduce you. This is Abigail Chase, one very wealthy widow. Old Abigail here, she did all right for herself. Went from running her own dinky little catering business to managing the entire food operation for Chase resorts. And then topped it off by marrying the boss."

He fixed a hard, studying stare on Abby. "I think you must be a lot smarter than you look, Abigail. You couldn't lose, could you? And old Taylor, he couldn't win. First, you cheat him out of a big chunk of his inheritance by marrying his brother; then, Roger decides to cut him out of the will altogether. Nice and neat."

"And that's where you came in, isn't it?" Daniel said from

174

his chair by the window. "You were supposed to make sure the will never got changed—and get rid of Abby and Chase's granddaughter in the process."

Catchside turned to him. "Ding-ding, blind man, you figured it out. And if you got that much, you probably know why I'm here." He looked at Daniel with a trace of scornful amusement."

"So Taylor Chase can collect on the will. Which he can't, until Abby's. . .death. . .is legally established," Daniel said grimly. "But just how do you intend to go about proving she's dead without implicating yourself?"

The contempt in Catchside's expression deepened. "Simple. The rest of you get this"—he lifted the gun—"and a trip down the river. But Abigail, she gets special treatment: a quick, clean drowning. Later, someone'll find her washed up on the riverbank, with proper identification—which I just happen to have with me." He sneered, tapping the pocket of his black shirt. "And I'll go back to being the man who never was."

Rocking back on the balls of his feet, his mood did an abrupt shift as he growled at Jennifer, "I thought you said the other two would be back soon."

When she nodded grudgingly, he stared at her for another few seconds, then snarled, "Get up. Maybe by the time I'm done with the three of you, they'll be here."

Not moving, Jennifer's gaze went from his face to the gun.

"I said *move!* Now! We're all going for a little walk down by the riverside."

Clutching Abby's hand, Jennifer helped her get up from the couch. Her own hands were shaking violently, but she faced him. "What are you going to do?"

He looked at her. "You want to know what I'm going to do?" he repeated with a contemptuous smirk. "See this gun?" He pointed it directly at her head and said softly,

"Bang-bang."

Jennifer jumped back, her heart thudding sickly as he leveled the gun at Daniel and silently mouthed the word again.

"Then you'll just get... washed away. Fish food. And when Donovan and the writer show up, they'll join you. Well, Donovan anyway." He stopped, adding with a different kind of smile, "I may want to talk to the lady writer a while first."

"*No. . .*" The sudden wail of protest came from Abby.

Catchside looked at her. "Sorry, Abigail, but that's how it is. Come on, now, let's get moving. I'm totally sick of this mudhole town. The sooner I can split, the better."

"Just how do you expect to get out?" The quiet, deliberate question came from Daniel, who had risen from his chair and was standing near the window.

Catchside whipped around, staring at him. "What do you mean, how do I expect to get out?" he mimicked nastily. "The same way I came in, jerk."

Daniel shook his head. "Wrong. There *is* no way out." His voice was unnaturally soft as he went on. "All the roads are closed by now. Most of the town is under water. And the dam's expected to collapse any minute. You're trapped. Just like the rest of us."

Jennifer stared at her husband in confusion. He sounded. . .peculiar. He was almost smiling, a baiting, scornful smile that wasn't at all like Daniel.

Catchside's eyes darted to the window. Licking his lips nervously, he snapped, "Shut up, blind man."

"It's true. You're not going anywhere."

Enraged, Catchside took a step toward Daniel. "*I'm* going anywhere I want to, jerk! *You're* the one who's not."

Daniel uttered a short, explosive laugh of contempt. With a roar of fury, Catchside lunged for him.

"*Jennifer—get out! You and Abby, get out of here!*"

The reason for Daniel's odd behavior crystallized. This was what he'd *wanted*, to goad Catchside into jumping him so she and Abby would have a chance to get away.

Frozen, she felt Abby sway, then break free. Before Jennifer could stop her, Abby threw herself at Catchside, grappling for the gun. At the same time Daniel pitched forward, slamming into the giant's back.

Catchside staggered, then planted himself hard in place, firing the gun in the air.

With an inhuman fury, he attempted to throw Abby off, but she clung to him, clawing at his face as she tried to wrench the gun free of his hand.

Jennifer lunged to help just as the gun exploded again.

Abby reeled, then fell. Screaming, Jennifer dropped to her knees, watching in horror as blood spread across Abby's shoulder, soaking the fabric of her dress.

Frantically, Jennifer looked around for something to stop the blood. Seeing nothing, she ripped the cloth belt of her slacks free, tore the lace curtain from the window and tied a piece of it around Abby's shoulder.

She turned around in time to see Catchside throw Daniel off, and level the gun at his chest.

"No!" With Abby still in her arms, Jennifer screamed a cry of warning. Daniel stopped, and Catchside swung the gun toward Jennifer.

"Try it again, blind man," he said, his voice a menacing growl, "and I'll kill you both right here, right now."

Daniel lifted both hands in the air, palms outward, in a gesture of surrender, then stood without moving.

Keeping the gun on Jennifer, Catchside ordered, "Get up." His small, glazed eyes were almost bovine in their lack of feeling.

"She's hurt, I can't—"

With one step, he moved to yank the semi-conscious

177

Abby roughly out of Jennifer's arms, tucking her to his side as if she were a rag doll. "I said. . .get. . .up."

Jennifer stood, shivering in fear, unwilling to let him see her cower.

"We're going to the river," Catchside said almost tonelessly. "Get a hold of your husband," he ordered Jennifer, motioning toward Daniel with the gun. "The two of you do exactly what I tell you to do, or I finish the old lady now."

Jennifer took a jerky step toward Daniel, then another. Touching him with a trembling hand, she felt the muscles of his forearm tense. His voice was hard and angry as he warned her, "Just do what he says."

They left the cabin. Jennifer and Daniel in front, Catchside behind them, dragging Abby lifelessly along at his side.

When they reached the bottom of the steps, Jennifer stopped, choking out a cry of despair. Sunny was still sprawled limply in the wet grass, her eyes closed.

As if he had seen, Daniel again squeezed her hand. "Sunny?" he asked in a whisper, squeezing her hand on his arm.

"Yes. Oh, Daniel. . ." She broke off, unable to finish.

"She's dead, isn't she?" he asked dully.

Jennifer's eyes burned with unshed tears as she turned to Catchside. "Please. . .let me see about the dog."

"The dog's dead! Now move!"

She had never seen the kind of anger that surfaced in Daniel, an anger she knew to be fed by grief for his beloved Sunny as much as his fury toward Catchside. Surprised, she felt him press her arm and grate under his breath, "Don't give up, Jennifer. Just don't. . .give up."

"Oh, Daniel. . .there's nothing we can do," she whispered. "He's *huge*—"

"—the Lord's bigger. And He's on *our* side."

"*Shut up*—both of you!" The gun punched Jennifer in the

178

back, and she stumbled.

Fear and hopelessness poured over her as the gunman prodded them down the thickly wooded hillside to the riverbank. Once she started to pray that Mitch and Freddi would return in time to help, but her prayer faltered. She no longer believed that even all of them together could stop this insane monster. Why pray that Mitch and Freddi be endangered, too?

At the bottom of the hill, Catchside stopped, motioning them with the gun toward an immense ash tree.

Keeping the gun trained on them, he began to drag the now unconscious Abby closer to the edge of the riverbank. The ground sloped down several inches toward the water, but the swollen, turbulent river was spilling across the bank, shooting up and over the small rise of mud-slicked ground above as it gathered strength for its descent to the valley.

Hauling her to the very edge of the bank, Catchside stooped, grasping Abby by the waist as he started to drag her to the water with the clear intention of drowning her.

Unexpectedly, she roused and twisted in his arms, throwing him off balance. Stumbling in the mud, he shoved Abby toward the water as he slipped.

Pushing away from the tree, Jennifer cried out as she saw Abby stagger and reel backward, clutching wildly at Catchside to save herself. The force of her weight pulling at him on the slippery bank was enough to throw the giant. He staggered, then pitched forward, dropping the gun as he toppled over and crashed into the water.

"Daniel—they fell in! Abby's too weak—she'll drown!"

Daniel was already moving. Ripping his shirt from his body, then tossing his shoes, he groped for Jennifer's hand.

"I'm going in—you'll have to try to guide me from here!"

"No, Daniel, you can't—"

"Just take me to the edge of the bank!"

Still Jennifer hesitated. When he started to step out on his own, she reluctantly guided him to the water's edge.

He stood listening for a long, tense moment. "Where are they?"

Jennifer looked from Daniel to the river. Already drifting out, away from the bank, Abby seemed to be just barely keeping herself afloat. Only a few feet away, Catchside, his face set in a look of shock, bobbed heavily in the water.

Jennifer turned to Daniel. His face was taut, his breathing shallow. He was poised, obviously waiting for her to prompt him.

She glanced down at the cotton slacks she was wearing. Making her decision, she pulled her blouse free from the waistband and kicked off her shoes.

"I'm going in with you." The steadiness of her voice amazed her.

When Daniel hesitated, she knew what he was thinking.

Jennifer wasn't a good swimmer. She wasn't even a fair swimmer. It was a family joke, her lack of prowess in the water contrasted with the skill of her Olympian husband. But Daniel needed her eyes. And Abby needed Daniel.

"The Lord has a way of putting us exactly where He wants us. . . ."

As Daniel's earlier words echoed from somewhere in a distant recess of her mind, Jennifer suddenly saw the truth of them. She was. . .*in the right place, at the right time.*

At that moment everything around her seemed to freeze and hang suspended, allowing her to view herself from an entirely different perspective. Without understanding how, she realized the Lord was giving her this instant, this brief blink in time, to catch a glimpse of herself as He saw her. . . standing where He wanted her to stand, being what He wanted her to be, doing what He wanted her to do.

180

Standing in His will. . .right where He had placed her.

I understand now, Lord, I really do. I don't have to do anything great or fantastic or newsworthy or world-changing. . .just as long as it's pleasing to you, Lord. . .just let me be pleasing to you. . . .

Taking a deep breath and a firm grip on her husband's hand, she began to move. "Now, Daniel!"

He hesitated only an instant, then sucked in a breath and went off the bank, surging left as soon as he hit the water. Jennifer followed him, determined, in spite of her fear.

"Stay to my right if you can," Daniel told her, pulling easily through the turbulent water. "Does he still have the gun?"

"No—he dropped it when he fell in!" Jennifer had all she could do to stay with him. The water was cold, dangerously cold for a poor swimmer, and the current seemed to be picking up momentum every second. Her legs felt sandbagged, and her arms were already beginning to ache.

"Are you all right?" Daniel was pulling away from her.

"I can't keep up with you!"

He slowed his stroke. "How far away is Abby?"

Jennifer squeezed her eyes shut against the sting of the water, then opened them. "Not far. I can reach her."

She shot a look at Catchside, surprised to see that he didn't seem to be doing as well in the water as *she* was. He was still several feet away from Abby, swimming haltingly, awkwardly, as if something were pulling him under. Those heavy boots couldn't be helping, she thought.

The water was full of wood, stones, and other debris being carried by the current. Jennifer screamed when a large, heavy tree limb caught Abby on the side of the head. The older woman's arms swept out once, then went limp.

Seeing his chance, Catchside pulled through the water

until he reached her.

"He's got her! Daniel—I think she's blacked out!"

"If I can pull him off her, do you think you can get her out of the water?"

"I'll. . .try." Jennifer was gasping for air now. She was already tired, more tired than she wanted him to know. And the raging current was quickly forcing all of them farther away from the bank, downhill.

Out of the corner of her eye, she saw an enormous chunk of wood rolling toward her. Swerving and cutting right, she watched it hurtle by, missing her only by inches.

"Glide as much as you can," Daniel warned. "Don't try to fight the current. Just keep moving toward them and let the water carry you. I'll try to get behind him, but you'll have to help me."

Jennifer's lungs felt seared, and there was pain shooting the entire length of her body. She couldn't answer him.

They were almost on top of Abby and Catchside now. Watching their approach, Catchside tried to turn and pull away, pushing Abby's head under water as he moved.

"No-o-o!" Jennifer fought for the strength to reach Abby. "Daniel—to your right! *He's to your right!"*

Turning, Daniel shoved off, circling behind Catchside as smoothly as if he could see.

Like a huge, primeval sea monster, Catchside bobbed up, then down, his eyes bugging when Daniel grasped him around the neck from behind.

Seeing her chance, Jennifer summoned all the strength she had and surged toward Abby.

Daniel had the giant by the throat, kneeing him in the back. Although Catchside had an obvious advantage in size, he was clumsy and uncertain in the water while Daniel's strength increased. He was already in control.

Grappling for Abby's arms, Jennifer ducked Catchside's fist as he tried to shove her away with one hand and to throw

182

Daniel off with the other.

Wrapping Catchside with both arms, Daniel shouted, "Take her, Jennifer!"

Wresting Abby free, Jennifer pulled her into a headlock. "I've got her, Daniel!"

"Get out of here! Hurry up!"

Jennifer bobbed uncertainly. "I'm not leaving you—"

"You've *got* to! *Do it*, Jennifer! While you've still got the strength! Don't try to swim against the current—go downriver and float toward the bank!"

Knowing she had no choice if she didn't want to risk both her life and Abby's, Jennifer began to swim. "I'll come back, Daniel!" she called out as she turned. "Just as soon as I get Abby out of the water, I'll come back!"

"No!" he roared, his face contorted with the effort of trying to keep Catchside subdued. "You'll be too tired! I won't be able to find you in this current! Stay on the bank!"

Jennifer hesitated, watching with fear as Daniel fought to keep Catchside from breaking free. Finally, with one last look at her husband and the madman in his grasp, she unwillingly pulled right, letting the current help carry her as she began to tow the lifeless Abby to safety.

It was like trying to uproot a mountain. A mountain in the sea. For the first time in his life, Daniel felt small. This lunatic was going to kill them both unless he could, somehow, knock him out.

The guy was *immense*! And crazy-mad! Daniel knew an instant of raw panic when the enraged giant pulled them both under water, hurling them against the torrential current of the river.

His own strength was beginning to drain when he finally managed to surface, still clinging to the struggling Catchside. Shooting upward, Daniel crashed down on the giant, riding him as if he were some kind of sea animal, trying

183

to push his head down into the water at the same time.

His own head felt as if it were going to explode any second. The roaring in his ears swelled to an almost unbearable pitch, and he was gasping for air as he tried to keep Catchside's face in the water.

. . .Save me, O God, for the waters have come up to my neck. . .I have come into the deep waters; the floods engulf me. . . .

The colossus beneath him began to buck in the water, trying to throw Daniel off. Shaking like a crazed bull, Catchside pitched and lunged, but Daniel held on, afraid to free a hand even long enough to throw a punch for fear he'd lose control.

. . .I am worn out calling for help. . .deliver me from those who hate me, from the deep waters. . .answer me quickly, for I am in trouble. . . .

He *was* in trouble. His legs were cramping, his arm muscles knotting, his lungs rebelling against the torturous pressure in his chest. He could feel the increasing sweep of current, as wood and other debris rushed past them in the water. He knew this end of the river was swelling from the effect of that extra cut-through at the dam. He had all he could do to hang on to the madman beneath him.

Dimly he realized a difference in the cacophony of the river; the roar in his head had changed. It wasn't in his ears at all, but rose from the water. His head snapped around, and a fresh pull of energy swept him upward.

For an instant he thought he might be about to lose consciousness, that he'd only imagined the sound. . . . He shook his head, trying to clear it.

No. . .it was real.

The roaring in his head had become the sound of a power boat.

Somebody yelled. "Hang on, Dan! We've got you!"

Mitch?

184

There was a hard *thwack* nearby, and he felt Catchside slump slightly beneath him.

Daniel realized now he was hearing not one engine but *two*. Both close by.

Now a different voice yelled out. *"This is the police! There's a gun on your head, mister. Give it up! You're under arrest!"*

Daniel felt somebody grab him under his arms and start to haul him up, out of the water and into the boat. He tried to help but couldn't seem to move his arms or legs. After a lot of puffing and grunting, he was pulled aboard and gently eased to the floor of the boat.

"Easy, guy. . .easy. . .we've got you." It *was* Mitch.

A gunshot boomed across the river's roar. Closer now, the unfamiliar voice again shouted. "I said, give it *up!* You don't get more than one warning!"

There was an ominous quiet, about the pause of a heartbeat, then, "They've got him, Dan! They've got Catchside!"

"Mitch—"

"It's okay." Mitch grasped his arm. "The police have him, Dan."

"The police. . .how. . . ."

"When Freddi and I got back into town, Tom Robbins was just getting ready to come up here. He'd been trying to call you, and when he couldn't get an answer at my place or Abby's, we grabbed a boat and started up the river. A couple of state policemen followed us up in another boat."

Daniel heard him catch his breath. "They've got Catchside in the other boat. Everything's okay, Dan."

Dan tried to push himself up. "*Jennifer—*"

"She's fine. She and Freddi are on the bank with Abby."

"Abby. . .is she—"

"Abby's all right. She's lost some blood, but she's okay.

185

Thanks to you and Jennifer."

"You're sure Jennifer is all right? She's not very strong in the water, and she sounded so tired—"

"She's *fine*, Dan. Honest. She's exhausted, but she's fine." Mitch stopped, then added, "She saved Abby's life."

"They made it. . . ." He could feel himself slipping, drifting off. . .he started to go with it . . .

Then he heard it. It was a sound as familiar to his ears as his own voice. In spite of the weakness, he forced his mind to focus—there—he *had* heard it.

"Sunny?"

Again came the bark. From a distance that could have been inches or miles, so rapidly was his consciousness shrinking, he heard her bark again.

". . .Sunny. . ."

"She's okay, Dan." Mitch's voice was no more than an echo, as if he were calling out from the other end of a long tunnel. "She's with Jennifer."

Daniel smiled, started to mumble a word of thanks, found his lips were numb.

It didn't matter. The Lord understood.

Epilogue

Friday evening

The entire hillside—above and below the campus—was covered with people and flickering lanterns.

From the platform which had been erected for the benefit concert, Jennifer could look out, past the crowds thronging the mountain, to see the town of Derry Ridge—what was left of it. The flood had left in its wake only mud, debris, and devastation. Though the additional spillway cut through the dam at the last minute had been enough to save the valley from annihilation, even those who had been fortunate enough to escape total loss had nevertheless suffered some degree of damage.

And yet they were here. *Everybody* was here, Jennifer decided, her gaze again sweeping the multitudes. They had gathered for a concert that would, hopefully, give encouragement to the audience as well as bring in vital funds to help rebuild.

Mitch and the festival committee, with Daniel's cooperation, had put together this last minute concert, turning it into a benefit event for the entire community. Much prayer and hurried planning had gone into the evening—with incredible results.

Jennifer had been in awe of Daniel's ability as a musician and a performer long before tonight, but never had she seen him capture an audience quite so quickly and completely as he had the thousands now spread out across the campus. It was as if God had chosen tonight to shed an additional supply of power and blessing upon her husband's music ministry, a ministry that had already reached countless

...earts throughout the country.

As she watched, both Daniel and Mitch came back onto the platform for the concert's conclusion. Along with the other singers and musicians, Jennifer stepped forward, then went to stand beside Daniel.

She exchanged smiles with Freddi and Abby, both seated as close as possible to the makeshift stage. Abby's arm was in a sling, but she looked wonderful.

It had come as no surprise to Jennifer that Abby's recently reacquired fortune was going to make little difference in her simple lifestyle. She had just that morning revealed her plans to all of them: to remain right where she was, in the cabin she loved, continuing with her work in the cafeteria. Her only concession to the Chase legacy was a suggestion to Mitch that she might want to add an extra room or two onto the back of the cabin.

"... So my grandchildren can spend weekends with me as often as they want," she'd explained.

"You have *grandchildren,* Abby?" Mitch had questioned with a startled look.

"Well, not *yet,* dear." Abby's glance had darted to Freddi. "But I should imagine I will *eventually.*"

Jennifer's eyes went to Freddi, fancifully imagining her in bridal white, since that's most likely what the stunning young author would be wearing when they next met. The wedding would take place early in the fall, Mitch had announced just before the concert. "*Very* early in the fall," he'd stressed with a challenging look at Freddi, who had merely grinned a silent assent.

Jennifer's smile faded for an instant at the fleeting, unpleasant thought of Floyd Catchside who, she thought with grim satisfaction, would never murder anyone else once the courts were finished with him. Not only was he being held for the murders of Roger and Melissa Chase, but law enforcement agencies throughout the country—throughout the *world*—were lining up to question him about numerous other unsolved killings.

The sound of Daniel's voice roused her from her thoughts, and she turned toward him as he spoke.

". . .I know there are hundreds—*thousands*—of you out there tonight who have lost either all your material possessions or at least a number of them."

Moving a little closer to him, Jennifer could sense the burden on Daniel's heart as he hesitated. But when he spoke again, his voice was firm and strong.

"While we were trying to put together this concert, I asked the Lord to give me some word of hope, some message of encouragement for those of you who need it most. Just this morning, I remembered something Mitch Donovan said to me our first day here. It's a line that I imagine many of you have already heard." He paused, then went on. "And it's a truth that once sustained me through a loss of my own—the loss of my sight.

"Tonight, I just pray that the Lord will write it on our hearts again, so we can draw on it throughout the days ahead—difficult days for many of you—and through all the days after that, whenever we need to be reminded of our legacy in the Lord."

The mountain was hushed as Daniel's voice rang out strong and clear. "Sometimes," he said, smiling with love at the people he could see only in his heart, "sometimes you have to get to the point where Jesus Christ is all you *have*. . . before you realize that Jesus Christ is all you *need.*"

The words drifted off into the night fog now softly enveloping the mountain. After a moment, Daniel began to sing, and soon the night rang with thousands of voices lifted in faith and hope . . .

"On Christ the solid Rock I stand;
All other ground is sinking sand . . .
All other ground is sinking sand."

189